Melissa Troy ✓

Dear Reader:

Everyone here at JOVE and all our authors are simply thrilled by the enthusiastic reception you've given to SECOND CHANCE AT LOVE!

We have lots of marvelous love stories coming up for the fall and winter by both seasoned pros and the brand-new talent we're very proud to be able to present. Our goal is to give you wholesome, heart-warming, yet exciting romances that are a pleasure to read. So, of course, your opinion about how well we're doing is very important to us, and we love to have your reactions to our SECOND CHANCE AT LOVE novels. Do let us hear from *you*!

Again, thanks for so warmly welcoming SECOND CHANCE AT LOVE. Your response has encouraged and inspired us.

With every good wish,

Carolyn Nichols

Carolyn Nichols
SECOND CHANCE AT LOVE
Jove Publications, Inc.
200 Madison Avenue
New York, New York 10016

"Hadn't we . . . better go back?"

Val asked, her voice quavering.

"I wouldn't want you to make any hasty decision you'd be sorry for later."

Nick was amused by her ambivalence. Mocking her. She sat very still, conscious of a wild desire to punish him, yet conscious of something else—a craving, painful as hunger, to prolong this moment, this closeness, this night, forever and ever.

"Hell!" he swore abruptly. Then he was on the ground with her, she in his arms, body calling to body with frightening urgency, such a weakness spreading through her that she was incapable of resistance.

Second Chance at Love™

MOONFIRE MELODY
LILY BRADFORD

A JOVE BOOK

First Jove edition published September 1981

First printing

"Second Chance at Love" and the butterfly emblem are trademarks be-
longing to Jove Publications, Inc.

Printed in the United States of America

Jove books are published by Jove Publications, Inc.,
200 Madison Avenue, New York, N.Y. 10016

Chapter One

VALERIE SHEPPARD DROPPED the phone to the cradle and groaned, "Oh, no!"

At the rear of the tiny shop, Deirdre Pennington glanced up in the act of separating Simba the cat from the tropical aquarium.

"Let me guess. That was Aunt Emily. And dear Patty is—"

"In love again!" Valerie sighed, her violet eyes crinkling at the corners.

"And you're elected to do something about it. I hope you said no."

Tall and slender, Valerie closed the distance between them in the small shop in only a few strides, and stood closer to her friend. "Oh, Dee, don't be silly. How could I? After all Emily's done for me? And this does seem a bit more serious."

Deirdre laughed, taking a sideswipe at Simba, who returned the compliment in the same coin. "All right, darling, if you must! Grab a cab and dash on over to wherever she is. But when you've pried her loose from the villain's clutches, will you please hurry on back? Between protecting your fish from this monster and waiting on your customers,

1

to say nothing of trying to get my paintings ready for the show, my head's whirling. How long will you be?"

"Dee," Val began, and hesitated. But there was no way, she decided, that she could break this news without precipitating an explosion. She took a deep breath, pulled back her long, shiny black hair, and forged ahead. "Uh—I can't get there by cab, Dee."

"By what, then? Bus? Train?"

"A plane, maybe?"

"A plane!" Dee gasped. "Good heavens, Val, where do you have to go?"

"Well, how does Utah sound to you?"

"Utah!" Dee came barging through the jungle of tropical plants. "Why on earth Utah?"

"Because," Val answered in a small voice, "that's where Patty Linwood fell in love—this time."

"I don't believe it."

"I wish I didn't have to. I'm just happy it wasn't Hong Kong, or Outer Mongolia!"

"Huh! You'd volunteer to go there, too, I suppose."

"Oh, but if you'd heard Aunt Em. She was hysterical!"

"Well, she certainly brought it on herself. The way she and that late husband of hers spoiled the girl rotten. Why on earth doesn't she go after her herself?"

Val laughed dryly. "You've just about said it. She knows she can't handle her. And unfortunately, it seems I'm the only one who can. Patty's histrionics leave me cold!"

Deirdre ran a hand through her close-cropped curls, such a strong contrast to Valerie's silken, dark locks, and shook her head resignedly. "Okay, I'll look after your shop and all the tropical plants while you're away. I always do. The Rain Forest will open for business every day as usual. And I shall feed that worthless cat of yours, too. And I'll keep our apartment shipshape upstairs the way you like it. And I suppose"—she paused, shooting Val a sly glance—"while I'm doing everything else, you'll want me to look after *Barry*, too, dear?"

"Barry!"

"Yes, Barry. I was wondering when you'd think of that?"

"Oh, Dee, I've been thinking of nothing else from the minute Aunt Em said Utah. I feel *destroyed!* Barry and I had so much planned, with his children coming in a few days."

"His children. Oh, yes! His children, by all means."

"Dee-ee-eee..." Valerie's tone sounded a warning. "I don't like that. If you weren't my dearest college friend—"

"I know."

"And if we didn't get along so well in the same apartment—"

"Hear, hear!"

"And if you hadn't always helped in my shop when I needed you—"

"All *right!* I consider myself chastised. And shall hereafter keep my large mouth shut about certain people. What were you about to say?"

Val drew a deep breath and exhaled with restraint before she answered, "Only that I'm not going to waste a lot of time out there pleading with my kooky little cousin. I figure I can fly out, get my hands on that girl, if need be wring her neck to keep her quiet, then fly straight back. Actually"—beginning to feel more cheerful—"I needn't be gone more than, oh, two or three days at the most."

"Lots of luck!" Deirdre shrugged.

"Thanks. Oh, Dee, you're a darling."

"I know. So what's your first move?"

Valerie was already into it. She whipped off her gardening smock just as a customer entered, and murmured hurriedly, "I'll dash up to Aunt Em's—she's waiting—and get all the details. Then I'll drop in on Barry on my way back. You can take over."

She smiled at the customer, hung her smock on its wooden peg, snatched up her handbag and raced to the street to hail a cab, casting a loving backward glance at The Rain

Forest, that tiny, lush, green gem of a shop brimming to the sidewalk with tropical plants that had become her life...after Barry Raynor first walked out of it.

At the corner of Grove and Bleecker, she picked up a taxi and heading uptown thanked her lucky stars there *was* a Deedee Pennington for times like this. Aunt Em had been downright incoherent. In fact, Val decided, beginning to sort the thing out in her mind, Aunt Em sounded exactly like Aunt Em when *anything* went wrong. It was not the first time Valerie had had to rush up to the brownstone in the East Eighties. Usually, she had been able to settle whatever it was with a kind but firm, "There now, darling, it'll all iron out." Though, as she acknowledged now, Val well knew that with seventeen-year-old Patty Linwood, nothing ever really got ironed out; it only got new wrinkles.

This latest wrinkle did indeed sound more serious when Emily had burst out with, "It isn't that she's done it again— f-fallen in love—it's who she's done it *with!* I don't know *what* he is. She doesn't say. She's just threatening to go off with him, *m-m-married or not!* Just to go off! Oh, Val, she's never threatened that before, I'm so afraid she might. She's so headstrong, and foolish, and impulsive..."

In spite of herself, Valerie had had to quell a moment of mirth. Aunt Emily, without realizing, was describing herself as a young girl. How well Val remembered her own mother, Emily's older sister, telling of their parents' be-wilderment over this fluffy-headed child of theirs, so dif-ferent from her siblings. "Whatever will become of her?" they used to say. "She's so *flighty.*"

To their everlasting astonishment, and everybody else's, Emily had run off and married at twenty an older man who adored her, laid the world at her feet, which he could well afford to do, accepted the daughter she'd borne him as if indeed Emily had been the first woman since Eve to perform such a miracle, and set out—with her help, to be sure—to coddle and indulge and spoil young Patty until she became, along with the glory, the very despair of their lives. And the carbon image of her mother.

Valerie, who had lived with the Linwoods after her parents lost their lives in an airplane disaster, had had ample opportunity to observe her young cousin Patty's mad capers. In the earlier years at Miss Young's School, Aunt Em kept beating a path to those premises to discuss Patty's endless falls from grace, which began at eleven when she locked Mademoiselle Lavalle, her French instructor, into a fifth-floor closet and tossed the key out of a window. The following year she distinguished herself, between milder infractions, by slipping off to poke about the city streets and shops, a small, inquisitive wraith, until she was quite ready to return, always with a tale of being "kidnapped by a handsome stranger," or, as in one case, having been picked up by an alert police officer and escorted back to Miss Young's, a horror that lady would take with her to her grave. But a final escapade which nearly resulted in expulsion began with her sudden appearance on the rooftop of the school building, where, in a fearless balancing act along the ledge, she delivered a virtuoso performance of a would-be suicide. The sole reason Miss Young did not strike her name at once from her roster of students was Aunt Emily's state of collapse which endured for more than a month. By the time of her recovery, Patty abruptly left all those hi-jinks behind her. Suddenly, at fourteen, she had grown up. She had discovered boys.

Looking back, Valerie often wondered whatever had led them to view this change in the girl with such welcome relief. In no time, never one for halfway measures, Patty began falling in love with the waxing and waning of the moon, until it was impossible to recall the names of the many boys who came stumbling through her life. All that remained, ringing in Valerie's ears, were the superlatives by which she described them—all Greek gods, to be sure.

Still, it was virtually impossible not to like the girl who was always so warm, and full of life and laughter, especially when things were going her way. For her part, among the people Patty adored, Valerie ranked number one. Reason enough, she reflected now as the cab neared her destination, for Aunt Em to turn to her and plead, as she had on the phone, that she talk sense to the girl. "You're the only one she'll listen to!"

Val had started to assure her, "But of course, Auntie, I'll be glad to. I'll phone her immediately—"

"But you can't!" Emily had wailed. "Don't you see, Val? She's way out there somewhere in the wilds. I told you, Utah, with this...this *animal!*"

"Animal? Who is he?"

"Nicky, she calls him in her letter. Nicky Mc-Some-thing...McKenzie, I guess. I don't know. I'm so upset. It's all so sinister. And the way she did it, sending that letter along with that little flybrain Bunny Hartman and the other girls who drove to the Coast with her. And just as blithely let her drop out there as if it were the middle of Fifth Avenue."

Valerie's head had whirled. "Auntie, start at the beginning. Start *somewhere, please,* dear!"

"Well, that was it. The girls were on their return trip. They came up through Arizona and into Utah. And that's where they ran into this man and Patty absolutely refused to budge from there. She sent back this letter. You should see it. I want to die every time I read it."

"Don't read it again, until I see you."

"She could have *phoned,*" Emily added, her voice breaking.

"Of course. I'm surprised she didn't."

"Oh, I'm not. She knew I'd never give her permission to stay on. Besides, the girls said she can't get to a phone. There's nothing near, apparently. I've checked that with the phone company. They say they've never heard of a place called Jordan's Hole! Oh, Val, you simply must go out there—at once, dear. There's no time to waste!"

That was when the shop had begun to spin around her, the plants threatening to throttle her with their thousands of shiny tendrils. For a bare instant, Val would have welcomed it.

At once? Now? Just as she and Barry had begun to reach

far into the past, gathering up those broken threads after
seven years apart? And to taste again those winy days that
once it had seemed no one could have taken from them . . .

For this upcoming weekend, they had planned a sail in
Barry's twenty-six footer on the Sound, a sort of mini-
vacation before the children should arrive. Val had looked
forward to it eagerly, with its dinner dance at the yacht club
later. She'd gone all the way buying a trim beige pants suit,
and a bikini over which she'd hesitated long and blushed
a little before plunging. The gown she'd chosen for dancing
had set her back at least a whole week's profits. But after
all those bleak years, it seemed right that she should be
doing it. Then on Sunday, there'd be a drive to Maine, with
dinner at some fabulous place Barry knew. There were so
many marvelous, exciting things Barry seemed to want to
give her now. Perhaps because he'd never been able to in
their early days. Perhaps to erase all the unpleasantness that
had blighted both their lives.

But now, oh, *darn* Patty anyway!

On an impulse, Valerie leaned forward and tapped on
the glass shield separating her from the cabbie.

"Yes, m'am?" he said, sliding the pane open.

"I'm sorry, but would you swing back down toward
Sutton Place? I just remembered—"

"Sure enough." He nodded and maneuvered for the next
turn.

Yes, I must see him first, Val decided, and get the bad
news over with. That wouldn't give them any time alone
together before Peter and Gillian arrived, but since they
could count on many weekends after the children had returned to their mother, it really shouldn't mean more than
a slight change of plans. Meanwhile, Val was fairly certain
she'd be back in time for the children's arrival. She was
very anxious to meet them; to get to know them well. She
wanted very much for them to like her, for the children
were beginning to loom up large in her life.

Idly, as the cab plowed southward, her hands began
pulling the pins from her long black hair, until the heavy

bun she wore at the nape of her neck fell in shining abundance across her shoulders. The way Barry had always adored it. "It's so beautiful," he used to whisper, adding, "*you're* so beautiful," running his hands through it.

Actually, she had not begun to put it up until it became a nuisance to work with around the shop. And when Deirdre asked bluntly one day if she were trying to captivate some nice elderly gentleman with poor eyesight and perhaps the gout, Val had shrugged. "As long as he can still see my plants, I won't worry about his gout or my hair, thank you."

Now, as the cab pulled up before the elegant Sutton Place address, Val shook the last of the loosened coil into a dark cloud and smiled at the double-take the driver gave her.

"Holy tomato, miss, I thought I'd switched passengers in midstream."

"Relax." She laughed. "Same girl 'before' and 'after.'"

When he was paid, Valerie hurried into the apartment lobby where the uniformed doorman bowed her to the elevator. She was no longer a stranger to him. He did not even have to announce her, not since Barry's path and hers had come together again on that magic winter night outside the St. Regis. She had just stepped from a cab, already late for dinner with Dan Ryder, a then-current date, and they had literally collided in her dash for the entrance before they *saw* each other. After that, she was *very* late meeting Dan in the lobby. But he'd been sweet about it, accepting her starry-eyed explanation about this chance meeting with an old, old friend. And she had been too breathless to elaborate. In fact, it would have been the poorest taste to try explaining how she and Barry knew, without putting it into so many words, that they were on the threshold of a fresh start. It was seven years, almost to the day, after Claire Drummond had snatched him away. But it was over now, all in the past, not to be dwelt on, ever.

Together, that's what they were. Together . . . again.

Now as the numbered dials flashed off the floors, Val's pulses quickened recalling Barry introducing her to the doorman that first time, making quite sure he understood.

"Charles, this is Miss Sheppard, and I'm *always* home to her. Just send her on up!"

And so it had happened, though, call it a small perverse streak in her, she had not fallen easily into his bed again. He had wanted her, and she him, urgently, both of them, but she had found a multitude of handy reasons to wait. She would have scoffed at any suggestion that she had grown wary, cautious, unwilling to risk a second heartbreak. She would have insisted it could not happen again; Claire Drummond was a once-in-a-lifetime disaster. And even if there were another lurking about, Barry himself was older, wiser, not to be taken in. Still, this time around, she had chosen to play it straight, so far. She was not about to guarantee, she thought, smiling, as the doors clacked ajar at the twenty-first floor, what this upcoming weekend might have brought about if *dear* Patty hadn't decided to be such a pain! Oh, well, perhaps it was best. She wasn't carved of stone, either, she conceded, flying down the hall to his door.

She was not surprised at the sound of voices mingling with low stereo music on the other side. It was an off hour for her to be visiting, and Barry had been using the apartment as an interim office while he was pulling his life back together, and his career. Predictably, Claire had left both in shambles. Oh, yes, there were people who insisted maddeningly that Claire had *handed* him his success. That were it not for marrying the "boss's daughter" Barry Raynor could never have made it so high, wide, and handsome in the brutal competition of the advertising world.

"Idiotic drivel!" Val always fumed at that. When she, a junior at Hofstra on Long Island, had first met Barry, he was already at the top of his senior class; a whirlwind of a man, a terrific mixer, a doer, an achiever! Sharing an off-campus apartment with him, after they knew they were in love and anything less than sharing quarters was hypocrisy, was like living in the heart of a tornado. What in the world could Claire, of all useless people, have handed him that he would not have gotten for himself? This butterfly with nothing on her mind but fun and games. Yes, and scheming and contriving to throw herself in his path every chance she'd had, with her rich, rich father cooperating, of course, until time after time it had been necessary for Barry to break dates with Valerie because Mr. Drummond wanted him present at a cocktail affair, dinner, or theater where important clients would be present—along with Claire, to be sure.

How simple it had been for her! For Barry, intent on business, seemed utterly blind to the girl's motive. Even when Val had teased him about it, saying "Well, if I were in her place, I'd probably be scheming and plotting, too. That is, until I knew that terribly attractive man assisting her father was *already* engaged to be married. Uh, does she?"

"Oh, come on, now, honey, we don't talk about my personal affairs."

"What do you talk about, darling?"

"Drummond Associates, what else? You forget, she's vitally interested in the concern. It's a family corporation, and she feels as responsible as her dad and her brothers for its success. And if anything"—here Barry had laughed—"the girl's just not my type. She's a bit too high-society for a working boy like me."

Of course she was. And yet, perhaps because Claire was going for "working boys" that season, somehow she did it, and scarcely a month after Barry's little declaration. How she did it, probably only Claire knew. Certainly Val would have sworn Barry was taken totally off guard. He'd been thrown into some embarrassing situation which left him no out. There had been a broken date again, then two.

Val, chafing alone in the campus apartment they had ceased to share after his graduation, blamed herself for not having moved to New York with him and commuted for her final college year. But it had seemed needless at the time. They had managed readily enough to be together several nights a week and every weekend, either in his tiny city apartment or in hers. They had managed marvelously well right up until Claire appeared on the scene. Then suddenly, it stopped working for them. There would come phone calls. He was "up to his eyeballs" in work. He couldn't afford the time. Mr. Drummond wanted him here, Mr. Drummond wanted him there, and "Darling, you've got to understand." More phone calls. More broken dates. "Tomorrow night, sweetheart." Promises, promises. And finally a waiting silence, during which time Val could not even contact him at his apartment.

The morning of the engagement announcement in the *Times,* he had contacted her at last. He had not been heartless. He had sent her a final note attempting to explain what could not be explained, vowing there had never been a girl like her. Nonetheless, it was over.

She might have accepted that, even weathered it better, Val supposed, if in less than a year, Claire hadn't started playing around again. Even after Peter and Gillian, their children were born, the gossip columns were full of her antics. She was here, there, everywhere except at home with her husband and children. And where was Barry? Working his head off and being father and mother as well. Eventually, it had to fall apart of its own crumbling weight, and that was when all the Drummond money bought a battery of lawyers to crucify him in court. The newspapers had had a field day...

At this point, Val invariably had to rip her mind away by force. Remembering was too ghastly. Those were the harshest of days. She never knew quite how she had finished her senior year, but she had been glad to leave college and all the painful memories. Back with the Linwoods, she had wanted to see no one, and Aunt Em worried and fretted over her, declaring typically, "But darling, love is so...*lovely.* Surely it's worth another try?"

And heaven alone knew where Em found the slews of young men she was forever bringing around to enforce that wisdom. Sons of old friends, they were, but no matter. Val had little use for any of them and distinguished herself by letting them know it—for a time, that is. Until her aunt, who had never been stern with her before, confronted her one day and said, "Well, now, young lady! It's been four months since that person dropped you for that other person. Four months of feeling sorry for yourself is quite enough. Four months of swollen eyes is entirely too much. Have you looked in the mirror lately? You're getting lines where *I* still don't have them. Is that what you want to do with your life?"

Her message had penetrated, at least to the extent that Val realized she had become an emotional burden. She murmured, "I'm sorry, Auntie. I know you've tried. And those *were* nice guys you brought around—"

"Hang the nice guys!" Emily had retorted fervently. "For now, anyway. *You've* got to do something with yourself, girl!"

"I know," Val agreed. "I must look for a job."

"That or—Val, there's a tiny shop in the Village. A plant shop. My friend Eunice Bailey owns it and doesn't run it very well. She wants to sell out and go to the Coast."

Remarkably, Val's ears had perked up. A *shop*. Not just a job. "But I don't have any money—"

"You can pay me back," was all Emily said. And so The Rain Forest, with the little apartment above it, came to pass. With people moving in and out of Val's days, some of those people men, as Aunt Emily had intended from the start, knowing that as long as she kept thrusting dates at Valerie, the girl would resist. Let the dates happen—and they happened—and soon Val was finding her way back to reality.

There was Jeff Emery at first, the one who bought the gigantic Staghorn Fern and wanted to move in with her two months later, which ended that one. There was Dick Etlinger, with the Wall Street brokerage firm, nice, but no thanks. There was Gary Hartman, the art dealer; Greg Connor, the photographer; Lew Marshall, and forgive her, names she could no longer recall. There was, in those dragged out years, no shortage of men, only a shortage of *feeling*. Never one to whom she felt so physically magnetized that she would sleep with him. It was as if she'd felt all there was to feel, and given all there was to give, to Barry, her first and only love.

And how glad she was now, hearing the door chime, hearing his approaching step. Here now came her love again, the only man she'd ever really wanted.

Chapter Two

THE DOOR FLEW open and her smile froze. The girl, very blond, very pretty, and perhaps a trifle tipsy, called over her shoulder, "Barry! Is this someone you know? Or should I tell her to get lost?"

Barry appeared at once, his sandy brows drawn together in irritation, until he saw Valerie and smiled, holding out his hands to her.

"Come on in, darling!" He seemed totally unruffled. "Ivy, this is Valerie," he explained to the tall, ravishingly dressed woman. "She's my dearest, my oldest friend—"

"I thought *I* was." Ivy pouted. Val was beginning to see she was more than just a *trifle* tipsy. "You never told me you had a girl."

"I never told you a lot of things, my dear. Val, this is Ivy Ashley." Val nodded and gave her a slow, uncertain smile as Barry added, "Jon Ashley is a client, honey."

"You *wish*." Ivy giggled. "Jon Ashley's *going* to be a client, if I tell him, 'Jon, I like Barry Raynor, he's ni-i-ice!' Right now, Jon Ashley better be picking me up here like he promised or there just might not *be* any Jon Ashley!" She ended with a steely laugh that set Valerie's teeth on edge. Barry flashed her a sidelong look that told her he

14

couldn't wait to get rid of the woman. A small weight she hadn't realized was there rolled off Val's back. She smiled up at him reassuringly. "I hope I haven't come at a bad time, darling, but something came up—"

Ivy caught it and broke in. "Sure, it's a bad time. 'S'always a bad time when a girl's just beginning to make it with Mr. Terrific!"

"Ivy, please." Barry laughed uncomfortably.

"Ivy, please!" she mimicked and minced up to him, slipping an arm around his waist. "How'd *you* like it if you were just getting some action and—"

Again Val darted a glance at Barry, as if to assure him she understood it was alcohol talking. But Ivy intercepted and translated it cannily. "Ho! Bet you think I'm drunk!"

Valerie had to suppress a laugh as Barry stepped in. "Now, Ivy, dear, I have a feeling Jon has been delayed at his meeting."

"Jon's probably found a little tart somewhere."

Barry ignored that. "Would you like me to take you back to your hotel?"

Ivy stepped back from him slowly, teetering on her too-high heels. Then suddenly shifting her hostility to Barry, she muttered, "I can find my own way. I know when I'm not wanted."

Snatching up her bag from a chair in the foyer, she groped for the doorknob.

Val whispered, "Will she be all right?"

Ivy reeled around at that. "Don't you worry 'bout me, honey. You jus' worry 'bout yourself. You got plenty reason. And you, Barry, your new agency might just have to limp along without the Jon Ashley Ent'prises!"

When she'd gone, with a reverberating slam of the door, Valerie breathed, "I'm so sorry. Do you think she meant that? About Jon Ashley Enterprises?"

He'd been staring blankly at the door, his eyes slitted. Now, with a shrug of his broad shoulders, he admitted, "She could. She's half the Enterprises. It's big, too. Headquarters in Texas. But I'll get along. I always do."

"I came at a bad time?" It was a statement and a question, and it hung in the air unanswered until she added apologetically, "Something came up I had to see you about—"

"Sure, why not? I've told you any time you wanted to drop in. We'd had a business lunch together, Jon and Ivy and me. She trailed after me when Jon had to keep an appointment downtown. She told him to pick her up here. What was I to do?"

"Of course, Barry. Only I wish I'd known. I seem to have ruined something."

"Forget it," he said, and as if bent on changing the subject, reached his arms out for her. "Nothing's important as long as we have this."

He found her mouth, eager and warm and ready, and for a long moment Val's world trembled on the rim of ecstacy.

"Now then," he said, releasing her finally, "what's come up? It better be good. I got word the kids are coming earlier than I'd hoped. Tomorrow morning, as a matter of fact—"

"So soon!"

"Uh-huh, that's the way I felt. I really needed several days yet to square things away. It's going to be bedlam here. So what's the problem with you?"

"You won't believe this, but—"

"Uh-oh!" Then grinning, "I can see I'll need a drink to get me through. Can I fix you one, darling?"

"No, thanks. I've got to tackle Aunt Emily as soon as I've talked this over with you."

"Good grief! It's sounding more and more dire by the second." He poured a double bourbon and joined her on a settee.

"Darling, it's Patty again."

"Patty?"

"My cousin."

"Yes, Emily's kid. What's she done now?"

Val laughed uneasily. "It's what we're trying to prevent her from doing that's bothering us. She's fallen for some—some, well, some 'animal' to quote Aunt Emily. Out in the wilds of Utah someplace. She's threatening to go off with him—*sans* marriage—also to quote Aunt Em."

"So what's that got to do with you? Ah, I get it, you're elected to run her down and save her from a fate worse than . . ." He chuckled. "Come on, darling, that's your aunt's job, why you?"

She hesitated. "Barry, Aunt Em is all the family I have in the world. When my parents went down in that crash . . . I don't know what I'd have done without her. When her husband died, my Uncle Fred, I gave her as much comfort, I hope, as she'd given me. When you married Claire, Emily's shoulder was always there for me. And believe me, I kept it well saturated."

"A-ah, honey," he murmured, slipping an arm around her. "I should never have let it happen, I know it . . ."

"Barry, we weren't going to talk about that, remember? It was a terrible mistake, an awful interlude, but it was over the minute we collided in front of the St. Regis last winter, and I saw that look on your face that told me all I ever needed to know; that you'd never stopped loving me. Right then it was over, past, finished! But while it was bad, I'll not soon forget how good Emily was to me. And when I needed something to sink my teeth into just to keep sane, she came up with backing for my business. If not for her, there'd never have been any Rain Forest."

"But you've paid her back every dime she loaned you, love."

"Money, yes. But for some things, there's another kind of coin. And this is one of those things."

His fingers had been tracing small patterns on her bare arm. Now he stopped. "But of all times, Val!" he broke in, sitting forward. "We had so much planned. And the children, you wanted to meet them."

"I want nothing more. It's why I'm hoping to fly out there quickly and get this thing done. With luck I could be back in two or three days."

His mouth twisted in momentary exasperation and she added hastily, "I hate it as much as you do, Barry."

"You can't possibly, Val. Sure, it wouldn't have been

too bad if Claire hadn't pulled one of those tricks she's so famous for. She knew I wasn't to have the kids for several days yet. She just couldn't wait to dump them. She's off to one of her health spas again."

"Something wrong with her, Barry?"

His brows rode up wearily. "Isn't there always? As long as there are good-looking and highly available doctors to cater to her whims—for a price! When she runs out of those, it's off to the Swiss ski slopes. And you should see those blond instructor types!"

"But, darling, the poor children. I feel so awful for them. And I'm so anxious to get to know them well."

"Then dump this pursuit of the foolish virgin, Val, for Pete's sake. No, for mine! Stay with me. I just can't handle those little hellers alone. I'm afraid of them!"

"Barry! They're your own kids! They're only four and six years old and you can't handle them?" She laughed as if he'd made a joke.

But he said soberly, "It's really not that funny. I've got a desk full of work to clear up, a new business to get off the ground. I'm out making contacts every day. Today was a waste, all right," he tossed in bleakly. "Darn Ivy, anyway!"

"That was my fault," Val said.

"Not really," he answered, rather unconvincingly she thought. Then he shrugged, "Maybe it's not over. But the kids, what'm I to do with them while I'm out? I'd been sort of counting on you, maybe more than I had any business doing, considering your shop."

"Well, I could have taken them down with me for a few hours each day. But as it is, darling, can't you get some reliable woman to come in, just for a few days until I get back?"

"Ha! Would you care to know how many women have gone fleeing after twenty-four hours? Babbling to themselves? Picking lint out of the air? It's a one-way ticket to the funny farm, those two!"

Val giggled. "I don't believe it!"

"Like to find out? If you've got to go, for God's sake, take them with you!"

Val greeted that with a burst of laughter in which Barry readily joined. Then abruptly they were staring at each other as if the plausibility of it had descended on them both in a single swoop.

"I wonder!" she breathed.

"No, I was only kidding."

"Barry, *I'm* not! I think it would be a lovely trip. And a perfect chance to get to know them!"

"You'll regret it before you get out of the city!"

"Nonsense! Back home, I'll have you know, I was the most sought after baby-sitter in town! My specialty was turning devils into such angelic darlings, their parents thought I used witchcraft. No, Barry, I'm not a bit afraid of them, and I really do mean it. I'd love to take them with me. Though I'd rather do it by car. It would take longer, but it would give you time to clear up a lot of business—and give me time to really get close to the kids."

"Sounds terrific."

"One catch. You have the car. Can I borrow your Jaguar Sedan?"

"You can borrow anything I own, love. I taxi all over town anyway. It's yours!" He was exuberant now, and it was catching.

"Darling! I can't wait," Val cried, jumping up. "I'm so excited."

"Just don't stay away from me forever, honey!"

"Just long enough to make you miss me," she teased. "But seriously, I certainly don't intend to drag this out with my man-crazy little cousin. I'll give her all the time she needs to pack, like ten minutes, and we'll be on our way back."

Barry looked doubtful. "What if she won't come!"

"She'll come. Especially after I tell her *friend* out there she's under age, which she is and is obviously doing an excellent job of concealing. I think his ardor will cool very rapidly indeed."

Barry smiled. "I wish you luck, but if he gives you trouble?"

"I'll handle him!" Val said crisply. "I don't know how, but I'll find a way. Meanwhile," she continued, dropping down beside him again, "I'm enchanted with this marvelous chance to be with Peter and Gillian. I feel that's important now." Her voice was almost at a hush. He set his glass aside and pulled her into his arms. "So do I," he murmured. Her head fell to his shoulder, and for a time he buried his lips in her hair.

"It *is* important," he added after a while. "Because I do have visiting rights, and it's one of those things we're going to be stuck with from time to time."

"Stuck with?" She sat up again. "You don't mean that, Barry."

His eyes crinkled. "Of course not. There's only one thing I mean. I love you. I don't know what I'd ever do without you. Honestly, Val, there were days with Claire when I lived solely on memories of you. The sweet little things you did for me, like typing my papers at school, remember?"

She laughed softly. "And sewing on your buttons, and making you coffee when you were cramming all night, and shaking you awake in time for your early classes, and meeting you at the snack bar so you'd slow down long enough to eat—"

She broke off, her throat gone unexpectedly tight with pain. Memories, even sweet ones, can stab sometimes. And there'd been too much water under the bridge. "Barry, let's not talk about it. Do you mind?"

He held her close again. "I just want you to know I'll never let you get away again, my Val."

She was on the point of saying she'd never tried to get away the first time. But his lips made that impossible. And then the door chime sounded. He groaned. "Damn! Business as usual!"

"I was on my way to Aunt Em's anyway," she said, rising.

"Well, wait," he pleaded, "until I see who it is."

When he opened the door, it was a tall, strikingly handsome, though harassed-looking man. "Why, Jon!" Barry greeted him, startled. Then quickly, "Come on in. Val, this is Jon Ashley."

The two nodded indifferently as Ashley's eyes swept beyond them.

"Where's Ivy?"

"Ivy. Sorry, old man, I thought she'd have contacted you. She left here some time ago."

"What in hell for? She said I was to pick her up here."

"She, ah—" Barry hesitated and Ashley's lips thinned. Val saw the muscles in his cheeks working.

"Damn it, Raynor, you didn't give her anything else to drink, after all she had at lunch?"

"She didn't have much here, Jon. She wasn't bad."

"She shouldn't have had anything! And I still don't know why she didn't wait for me," Ashley said.

"I'm afraid she was a bit ticked off, Jon."

Ashley shook his head, the weary look back in his eyes. "She gets that way when she's tippling. I hope she didn't make a nuisance of herself."

"Don't worry about it, old man. We all have our moments, don't we? But," he added with a dry laugh, "she did say I'd lost your account."

Ashley's eyes riveted on Barry a second. "But why?"

"I'm sure I don't know, Jon. *Have* I?"

There was a moment's hesitation before Ashley answered, "No, of course not. I'll talk to her. She probably won't remember a thing about it. But I'd better be on my way. I'll have to run her down someplace."

Val felt sorry for the man after he'd gone. "Did you know she was that way when you offered Ivy a drink?" she asked.

Barry flushed. "Who offered? She helped herself. She's a lush, everybody knows that. So does Jon. But it's her money in the business—and do I ever know what that means!" He paused, his anger melting away. "Anyway, I don't seem to have lost the account after all."

"Are you sure you want it?"

"Why not? As Jon says, Ivy's probably forgotten all about it by now, and anyway, I've know her for years. She's an old friend of Claire's. Went to school with her. Ah-h, she's not so bad. Well, then, you're going, darling?"

"I'd better. I'll phone you later after I've arranged whatever's needed. And anyway, I'll see you, and the children, tomorrow. I can't wait."

"Nor I," he said and walked her to the elevator.

At the street level, alone, Val finally came to grips with something that had been nagging her from the moment she'd arrived. "This," Barry had told Ivy Ashley, "is Valerie, my dearest, my oldest friend."

Not "my fiancée." Not "my future wife." Not even, come to think of it, "my girlfriend."

Chapter Three

THERE WAS ENOUGH turmoil at Aunt Emily's to wash that minor irritation out of her mind. Emily was pacing the floors when Val arrived, her eyes puffy from crying.

"I'm so *glad* you got here, Val. Just look at this, that's her letter," she said thrusting a paper under Val's nose. "I'm beside myself. I was crazy to let her go with those girls in the first place. But they'd all just graduated, and she begged so hard. I never dreamed it would come to this."

"Okay, suppose I fix us some coffee and we'll sit down and talk."

"Talk? Val, you don't understand, there isn't time for talk!" Emily said, pacing again. "While we're talking, that kid can be getting herself raped!"

"Raped? But Em, this letter is three weeks old. Those girls certainly took their time getting back here with it. If Patty was to be raped, which I seriously doubt, I would think it's all over but the shouting. Somehow, she was still unraped enough to write you when she did, and if it's happened since, I don't see how we can undo the damage, do you?" She paused, then added guardedly, "Unless you want to go to the police?"

"The police? Good God! And see it in screaming head-lines all over the *Daily News*?"

"Then be reasonable. Remember, her girlfriends didn't seem upset, did they?"

"What do they know? Young girls. Heads full of fluff!"

Val suppressed a smile, remembering awkwardly her mother's description of Emily at that age.

"Come on, now, if they'd sensed danger, they'd never have left her there. Or at the very least, they'd have phoned you immediately."

She left Emily to mull that over and fled to the kitchen to put on the coffee. There she began reading Patty's letter.

"I'm in love at last!" That was her opening line, and Val shook her head in disbelief. Was it possible Patty had convinced herself this was the first time? After all those other declarations ranging back to that memorable fourteenth year when she had exchanged mischief for men? Between then and now, Valerie had stopped keeping score. It was all so meaningless anyway, she thought, reading again. A third of the way through, she smiled. Halfway, she giggled. Before she'd finished, she had to cover her mouth to keep from laughing out loud. Not that it was precisely a laughing matter, but Patty had a way of altering perspectives so that neither was it necessarily a crying matter.

What was really amusing her, however, was Patty's accompanying pen-and-ink sketches of her latest's male charms. "His arms, his muscles—like this!" And, "His back, the way it ripples." Then, at last, the nitty-gritty of what was killing poor Emily—"Mother. You never saw such hips on a man, and those thighs!"—all faithfully illustrated.

Val spun around as Aunt Emily spoke from the kitchen doorway. "See what I mean? Where did that girl learn about his hips and his thighs?"

"Come on, now, Em, darling."

"Val, please don't 'darling' me now. You know the answer to that one as well as I."

"But you're jumping to conclusions, Aunt Em. If he were

wearing shorts, she'd have seen them!"

Emily sniffed. "It's the *enthusiasm* that's worrying me. She doesn't say one word about the *man*, his character, his family, what he does for a living, where he comes from. He certainly didn't spring up fullblown in that wilderness! All she says is that she *wants* him! You read that?"

"Yes, yes, and she's going to follow him to the ends of the earth." Val sighed, unimpressed. "Em, dear, *you* know Patty."

"That's just why I'm so scared."

"Now you're being silly, Aunt Em. If there were anything really bad going on, do you think she'd have written the way she did, or the things she wrote?"

"It's what she left out that scares me, Val. I feel it's deliberate. Oh, you *must* go and bring her back!"

"If I can find the place."

"You shouldn't have too much trouble, Val. The girls left me directions off the main highways—after I threatened them with extinction if they didn't. Would you like me to go with you?"

Valerie thought not. "I can do better alone."

"Yes, that's the way I feel, too," Emily agreed, sounding relieved. "She won't listen to me." Then with a sigh, she added, "Young girls are so difficult these days. Oh, I know what you're thinking. Everybody used to say I was so flighty, but I wasn't ever *crazy*, Val, you'll have to admit. And even I settled down when I fell in love."

"Aunt Em," Val put in slyly, "isn't it just possible that that's what's happening to Patty? That she's finally found—"

"Love? *Her?* Val! She wouldn't know the real thing if she fell over it. Now you just get ready and fly to Salt Lake City—"

"I'm driving, Aunt Em. I'm borrowing Barry's car. You see, I'm taking his children."

"Barry's *children*! Whatever for? Won't they slow you down? Make it awfully difficult for you?"

"I doubt it. Anyway, it's either that or I can't go at all.

You see, he's—" She caught herself about to say "stuck with." "He's to have them for their court-ordered visit, you know, a bit earlier than he'd expected, and I'd been planning to help him with them. He's so weighed down now with work."

"Of course," her aunt agreed. Then she remarked thoughtfully, "You really do love that man, don't you, dear?"

"Adore him."

There came a tight little pause. Then she continued, saying, "You must. You've always done so many things for him." And without waiting for Val's comment, she asked, "When do you plan to leave?"

"Tomorrow, as soon as I've met the children at Barry's. Which reminds me, I have loads to do, Aunt Em. I'll just dash down to my place now and do a bit of packing. I'll stop on the way to gather up some toys and picture books in case the children get bored or restless."

Emily sighed. "There's very little chance that *you* will, Val. You have no idea what you're getting yourself into."

She meant the children, of course. But later Valerie could not imagine why her mind latched onto that comment with a shiver of premonition.

Unless it *was* Patty's silly little note that dwelt so shamelessly on the man's physical characteristics, as if she'd rather not discuss all the rest. And it was precisely what "all the rest" might be that was giving Valerie a moment's pause. What was the man like who hid away in a place called Jordan's Hole, too insignificant for any map, too obscure even for a roadside phone booth? Out of this sudden whirl of activity now loomed this faceless stranger who could be—anything! A shiftless hippie type? A fugitive from society? On the lam from a wife and children or AWOL from the army? Maybe some illegal alien? Val's hands went clammy ticking off the possibilities. Patty, on the other hand, concentrating on this stranger from the neck down, would hardly be deterred by such frivolous flaws in his nature, and for a second Valerie almost opted for the plane flight again. But reason triumphed. As she'd assured Emily, if the worst was to happen, it had already happened, no doubt. A few days either way could hardly matter any longer.

As the cab pulled up in front of The Rain Forest, she shoved all those ugly implications to the back of her head and ducked inside for a brief confab with Deedee, who shrugged when she heard about the children going.

"It's your life, Val."

"I know. And it thrills me! I'll go up and start packing. And again, you're an absolute dear to help me out!"

She patted Simba on his head, dodged his needle-sharp claws, and took the stairs at the rear of the shop as if airborne.

Valerie felt she had barely drifted off to sleep when the phone jangled her awake. Daylight. Eight-fifteen in fact. And Barry was on the other end of the wire. "They're here, Val. Claire's chauffeur just dropped them off!"

She blinked the sleep from her eyes and mumbled, "That's nice."

"Nice? I'm paralyzed with terror. Already!"

Val's yawn ended in drowsy laughter. "A great big father-type like you, terrified of your own little cubs?"

"Some cubs! They're nosing around to see what to get into."

"I don't hear anything."

"Give 'em time. Or better still, can you get here soon, honey? I've got a big day ahead."

For a fraction, Val restrained herself from reminding him that she had one, too. Stifling that, she said quickly, "Just let me shower and grab a cup of coffee. I'll be there in no time."

"I shall barricade myself, waiting." He laughed. "Sweetheart, whatever would I do without you?"

That's a good question, she thought when they'd hung up. Barry really did need her. He was such a funny, helpless sort of man; just great with big, important deals, but with

little things, and little ones, he didn't seem to know where
to start.

Smiling wryly, she headed for the shower, noting that
Deirdre and Simba had already descended to the shop below,
which in a way was good. The only times she and Deedee
ever clashed was over Barry. Dee, ever independent where
men were concerned, simply could not understand her de-
votion to him. And so it was better not to talk about it.

Half an hour later, Val stepped from a cab outside Barry's
place, breezed past Charles the doorman, unaware of how
her tall, slim but full-busted figure impressed him, and
hurried to the elevator, conscious of a sudden tensing at her
middle. She had been trying ever since waking to play down
that sense of having to measure up. For it was vitally important that the children should like her, far more than Barry
seemed to realize. There was very little doubt in her mind
that once they were married, Barry's children would be
spending more and more time with them, especially considering Claire's penchant for jetting around the world in
search of . . . whatever she was in search of. Women like
that! Valerie seethed, stepping out on Barry's floor.

She heard no sound beyond his door other than his steps
hurrying to admit her. "Love you for coming so fast!" he
greeted her. "Come on in, I'll pour you some coffee before
the onslaught."

"What onslaught? They're silent as mice. Have you glued
them to the ceiling or something?"

He laughed. "No, I sent them downstairs to play—"

"Downstairs! Barry, they just got here!"

"I know, I know. They didn't know what to do with
themselves."

"Of course not," she said softly. "You've—sort of got
to help them—"

"Charlie's helping them. He's got kids, too. He didn't
mind. For what I tip him, he better not."

Val blinked a couple of times. Yes, she recalled seeing
children on the walk talking with Charles. She hadn't really
seen them in her rush. Now, as Barry came to her holding

out her coffee, she said, "Leave it on the table, honey. I think I'll run down and bring them back."

"Oh, for heaven's sake, why?"

She hesitated. "Why not?"

Their glances grazed, and he finally shrugged. "Okay, if that's the way you want it. You don't have to go down. I'll phone the lobby to ship them back up."

For a nasty moment, her mind played tricks. This morning the chauffeur had "dropped them." Now the lobby would "ship them." She was glad when at least Charlie himself brought them to the door, holding each by a hand. They were barely inside when Peter, the older, whined, "Aw, we were having such a good time." Barry shot her a look that clearly implied, "What did I tell you?" But to the boy, he said, "Valerie wanted to meet you. Let go of Charlie's hand and come say hello."

"Aw-w-w," he protested, his bottom lip jutting. The little girl, Val noticed, was inspecting her with four-year-old candor. But as her brother's complaints grew louder, she whimpered, "I want to go downstairs, too."

"Well, you can't!" Barry said. "Okay, Charlie, thanks for bringing them up. Peter, Gillian, let go of Charlie's hands. Do as I say now! *Do you hear me?*"

The last was a roar, and abruptly they dropped the doorman's hands—in fear, Val thought, with a stab of guilt for having caused it all. As Charles backed out the door promising to play with them again, Peter turned a baleful stare on her, his eyes filling. Gillian followed suit like clockwork, and when the boy cried out, "We never have any fun," Gillian suddenly sobbed, "I—want—Mommy—"

For a shattering moment, Valerie felt crushed. Then Barry muttered, "Now do you believe me?"

Her violet, thickly-lashed eyes clashed with his an instant while she wondered why he didn't go to the child and comfort her, or find ways to distract her. The next minute she was doing it herself. She fell to her knees beside Gillian, an act that astonished the small girl into wide-eyed silence. "I was hoping so much to have fun with you and your brother, dear, before you go back to Mommy," she said. "I'd be terribly disappointed if you went so soon."

Her response was hardly instant sweetness and light, but there was at least a sign of appraisal in the child's eyes. Val took quick advantage. "Would you like to drive way out West with me, Gillian?"

Before she could answer, Peter came muscling in. "*I'd* like to go way out West."

"I *knew* you would!" Val said, still on her knees. On that level, they examined each other, eye to eye.

"I've got a cowboy suit," Peter announced. "Only I don't have any hat."

"Oh, you must have a hat. In fact, that will be our first order of business when we get there."

"I want one, too," Gillian cried.

"You can't have one, you're a girl!" her brother said.

"Of course she can! *I'm* having one!" Val announced. Then hugging Gillian, she added, "We women stick together."

Val heard Barry chuckle, but kept her attention on the children. Gillian's small face broke into sunlight as Valerie unveiled her plans. At one point, Barry stepped up to their circle, and Val became immediately aware of Peter turning his rigid young back on him, as if unconsciously blocking his father's advance. She knew the exact moment the whine entered the boy's voice again. It came when Barry playfully said, "Oh, boy, I wish *I* could come!"

"Not you!" Peter protested. "You're busy. You said so. *We're* going—Gillian and me—and—and—"

"Valerie," she prompted.

"Valerie," he echoed. "When do we start?"

"A-hah!" Barry teased good-humoredly, "You can't get away from your old man soon enough, can you, son? Aren't you going to miss me?"

The boy said nothing. The silence opened like a hole, and Valerie wished he would answer, *anything*, even if he had to lie, as an adult would have done. But Peter Raynor was six years old, at an age that doesn't fiddle with amen-

ities. His answer was straight to the point—a deafening
silence! When it became too much, she covered for him,
sending the children to play in another room.

"I have millions of things to do if we're to get started
later. Meanwhile, you two just go practice some Indian war
whoops!"

They took her literally, filling the rooms with such howls
and shrieks that Barry's face screwed up in pain.

"But, darling, they're only children." She laughed.
"What do you expect?"

"Just what I'm getting. A headache." He grinned.

"You're so—funny about them."

"And you're so lovely." His arms came around her and
she nestled there for a time. Thoughtfully.

"You're going to miss them when they're gone, Barry."

"Ah, honey, I'm so busy these days, I can just about
squeeze in time for missing you."

She was on the edge of saying, "I didn't mean 'these
days,' Barry." But his hands were at her temples, and then
they were in her hair, and his mouth on her lips, and the
thought was beginning to slip away...and so she let it
go...

Chapter Four

It was hot. The sun scorched like a furnace ever since they'd turned south from Salt Lake City, and Valerie could not imagine where the children were getting all their energy.

She could not imagine, either, how she could have gone off so blithely trusting the haphazard map that Bunny Hartman, under duress, had sketched for Aunt Emily. While still at Salt Lake, she had pored over it as the children slept in the South State Street motel, comparing it with the road map she had picked up along the way. She had thought it would be a snap. She hadn't counted on the distances, or on Bunny's utter lack of orientation. Or the towns the girl had named "Something-city, I think," or "Buffer, or maybe it's Puffer, and I think there's a Dale in there someplace." (Hadn't Aunt Emily called her "fly-brain"?)

Before giving it up to try for sleep, Valerie knew the only thing she could be sure of was that she was meant to head south, and eventually west, which looked fearfully barren on the official road map. She hoped to pick up clues along the line. And surely, if the girls had found a place called Jordan's Hole, it had to be there, and somebody would know about it—even if the maps refused to admit it.

Dawn + Reg
called, ~~call them~~
back.

Al

254-6091

Rob

966-0175

2989

Grandview

unit 2

She hoped she'd fall right off to sleep, but overly tired, she had tossed far into the night. Ever since New York, the children had been—well, children. High-strung, excited, noisy, demanding, just as Barry had predicted. But she'd prepared for it with a tote bag full of books and games. As it turned out, it was the only thing she'd been prepared for. She had been completely unprepared for Gillian's sudden burst of tears that first night together—*for her mother!*

"Shall we phone Daddy, darling?" Val had offered. "And you can talk to him?"

"*Not Daddy!*" the little girl had raged convulsively. "I want Mommy—Mommy—" Val had taken her into her own bed and hugged and fussed over her until she'd fallen asleep, out of exhaustion. Then she'd whispered across to Peter who'd watched large-eyed and silent, "She's all right now, dear."

He'd said nothing, and Valerie saw with a wrench that his eyes were also wet, and his pillow damp. And for a scant instant, her contempt for Claire's heartlessness slopped over on Barry, too. She hadn't been prepared for *that*, and stifled the feeling guiltily.

Far less easily stifled was awareness of those tiny children's enormous hunger for affection, a need so desperate that, knowing her scarcely a day, they had turned their young backs on their father, laid their trusting little hands in hers, and willingly, almost eagerly, allowed themselves to be led unquestioningly into some great unknown. Her mind harked back a very long time to when she was Peter's age, and her grandmother, whom she loved, had invited her for a whole summer's visit to her Uncle Larry's in Alaska, a prospect so dazzling to contemplate that everybody had been stunned when she declined. But she had been unable, even terrified, to imagine such time and distance between herself and her parents. Just as she was unable to imagine now what heaviness and hurt in those two young hearts had sent them without hesitation to her arms. Somewhere, there must lie an explanation. But for the present, she turned her mind away, because dwelling on it only raised more questions than it answered. Meanwhile, she was determined to make this journey a time they would never forget.

Once in Salt Lake City, the children's spirits soared again, their new, promised cowboy hats set jauntily on their heads. Breakfast over, Val had piled them into the car and nosed south. But there, too, she was unprepared for the breathtaking beauty through which they drove. The majesty of the Wasatch Range was like nothing she had anticipated. She had not been *thinking* in terms of scenery. Now she kept wishing she could loiter and take the side roads into the canyons that notched its flanks.

At Utah Lake, temptation was too much. The children begged her to stop and she was all too willing to give in. She swung into Provo to lay in supplies, then west again to the State Park. The picnic lasted well into the afternoon, and even so they were reluctant to leave.

Back, back as far as she could thrust them, went thoughts of Patty and her "animal." She lost precious hours of travel, and the "rescue" was that much deferred. Yet somehow, in the grandeur of these surroundings, as in the friendliness of the people everywhere, it was impossible to conceive of the fears that sprouted constantly in Aunt Emily's head. Anyway, one day more or less could hardly make much difference—to Patty, to Emily, or to a world of such ageless magnificence.

As she pointed the car townward again, her eyes lifted a moment to Timpanogos, that ancient ridge serene as a sleeping woman beneath a blanket of snow. It was omen enough to relax and enjoy; she could make up for lost time next day.

On the phone from the motel she'd found south of the city, she told Barry of the slight delay. He sounded disappointed.

"But I miss you, love."

"I do, too, darling. I'll rush it along after this. As much

as I can, considering that with Bunny Hartman's map, I feel like an early explorer. But it's south again tomorrow, and on to the lair of the beast!"

"And tell that kid cousin of yours I shall personally administer a paddling when you bring her home. She's robbed me of you, and I don't take kindly to that."

Val laughed. "Would you like to speak to your son and daughter? Or are you too busy? I hear voices in the background."

"Oh, just a few clients."

"Uh—Ivy?"

"No, thank heaven. All right, put the kids on."

But minutes later, she had to tell him, "They're under the bed and won't come out!"

"It figures." He chuckled. "Hope they're not being their usual nuisance?"

"They're being darlings, Barry."

"Then they're not my kids. You got 'em mixed up with somebody else's."

When they hung up, she smiled over that, thinking, he won't know them when he gets them back. But then, they were almost hers already.

"Come out, come out, wherever you are!" she sang to them suddenly and was rewarded with a delayed giggle. One after the other, they squirmed from under the beds and stood before her, grinning. "There you are!" she cried. "I didn't know what to tell your daddy when he wanted to talk to you."

"He didn't," Peter mumbled. "He only said so."

"But you're wrong, Peter. Daddy was disappointed." Even as she spoke, it struck Val she was lying; lying to the children because the truth was vague and unthinkable. And you can't make a child understand a man is . . . *busy* sometimes.

"He wasn't," Peter pursued when she would have let the thing drop.

"Aw, come on now, give your daddy a break. Why

would he say he wanted to talk to you if he—"

"He *didn't*, he *didn't*, he *didn't*, you *asked* him, we *heard* you!" He shouted the words, filled with anger. Would she never learn that children are sharp as tacks, their ears picking up things like radio antennas, catching every syllable, every inflection, even when they seemed not to be listening? She veered off the subject with a hearty offer of bedtime snacks which Gillian promptly accepted. Peter came more slowly to the table, his young face somber. He took his seat in silence and reached in silence for the dish of ice cream she had portioned out from the container in the tiny refrigerator. Val felt a hollowness opening in her middle, watching him with sidelong looks as Gillian chattered away. Then abruptly the boy said a thing that cut like claws to the heart, "He makes my Mommy cry and I hate him!"

There are times there is no answer, and this was one of them. But long after the children slept, she leaned over Peter to kiss him lightly on the temple. He did not stir, but gazing down at this child growing old too soon, her eyes filled. Why *couldn't* Barry see how he was blighting his relationship with his children? Why had he never sat down with them to explain in whatever words came from his heart how he, too, had "cried." And that they must not hate their mother because of it; just as they must not hate him for their mother's tears. Ah, yes, there was much room for change, Val knew, and once they were married, that change would come about. This much she vowed.

The following day, Valerie picked up a new route westerly toward the desert. She had dissected Bunny's map some more and discovered something marked "Confusion Valley." Was the girl being snide, she wondered, until she compared it with the official map and suddenly breathed, "Hallelujah!" It was the first name that coincided with anything on the road map. And there, in fact, was a road that led in the general direction, though the big X that Bunny had designated as her final destination seemed still to be well south of there, and apparently in the center of nothing. If there were paved highways leading to it, they did not show on the road map. It would be dirt roads, she decided, with vast distances between them. In an inspired moment before leaving Provo, she loaded up on food and thermos bottles of cold drinks for any emergency.

It was every bit what she had expected. The long stretches between tiny communities—sometimes hardly more than a general store with a couple of houses—amazed her, as did the sparseness of the population. And the heat was enervating, at least to her, though not to the children who at each rare stop leaped from the car and tore about madly. But the people she met and the tourists she flagged down to question were open and friendly and helpful, in every way but one. No one had ever heard of Jordan's Hole, though she'd criss-crossed from one dirt road to another and was finally beginning to understand why Bunny's map was so worthless.

The area was a bewildering maze of gullies with the road snaking along at the base of the cliffs that reared hundreds of feet to the sky. At one point, Valerie realized she was every bit as confused as the area's name suggested, and even more so than Bunny and her map.

At a place where two trails junctioned, she stopped the car to think. The children burst from it like the pips of an orange, and wonder of wonders, racing about, found a spring. There'd been nothing like it for many miles, and it kept them occupied long enough for Val to decide that, in the late-afternoon light, one of these dirt roads appeared to be better traveled than the other.

Herding the children back, she set off again, for she was growing apprehensive now about where they'd spend the night. For miles since the last small store, there had been nothing. But roads do not lead nowhere . . . or do they? This one, Val decided after losing all sense of direction, rambled along its winding way as if determined to do just that. And precisely at that moment she rounded a bend and saw straight

ahead a sign that made her sing out, "Finally! Now we're
getting someplace!"

The sign was ancient, the arrow pointing off to the left
all but obliterated. So, too, was the name beneath it:

JAKE JORDAN'S—One Half Mile.

With a surge of hope, Val hit the gas pedal again.
They've simply got to know something, she thought. Taking
a sharp turn, she found herself almost at once before another
of those general stores that seemed to spring up like oases
in the lonely barrens, though never, Val thought, as welcome as now.

Still, unlike those others along the route that were spot-
less and well ordered in the Mormon tradition, this one
appeared seamy and dilapidated. Her heart clutched with
disappointment, thinking it an uninhabited relic along with
the cluster of adjoining structures whose roofs were fallen
in and doors sagging, crumbling from disuse and neglect.

But then Val saw the lines of listless sheets and faded
garments strung across a littered yard at the rear of the main
building, and knew the place was alive after all. If the store
had ever seen paint, the last flake was apparently long fallen.
The front steps slanted perilously and the windows were
yellowed and cloudy. Yet signs nailed to the porch uprights
advertised the ubiquitous cold drinks, cigars and cigarettes,
chewing tobacco, and popular snacks. A low hum puzzled
her until she identified it as an electric generator. There was
even, she noticed, a telephone emblem posted beside the
door. But Valerie felt in that moment that the only thing
she would have stopped for if she were not looking for
Jordan's Hole would be gasoline from the lone pump which
apparently serviced the back-road traveler.

As she pulled up before it, the children made a lunge for
the door, but she stopped them. "We won't be here long,
just for gas and information. It's late and we've got to get
where we're going."

They protested, but sat back. And it was at this point

that Valerie glanced up to where a bony-thin woman with bloodless lips and colorless straggles of hair sat in a porch rocker watching her.

Valerie, waiting at the pump, was beginning to wonder if the woman was actually blind, when after some stony minutes, she called down, "You wantin' gas?"

"Yes, please."

The woman seemed to hesitate a moment longer, then yelled over her shoulder, "Jake? You comin' out? Lady wants gas."

Still nothing happened. The woman continued to stare until Val, having enough of it, got out from behind the wheel and started for the porch. She had reached the first step, when the screen door flung open and a man slouched from the shadows. He was unshaven and his torn shirt was stained with grease and sweat. "I'm comin'," he said querulously as he paused to lean a rifle against the wall at the woman's side. Shuffling on toward Valerie, his eyes swept her figure in a manner she found unnerving.

"Just fill it up, please," she said, returning to the car. "And you might check the front, too."

As he went about his job, grudgingly, she thought, she remembered to ask the all-important question. "Can you tell me how to get to a place called Jordan's Hole?"

Again she was met with that irritating silence, though she was certain he had heard. She had seen his eyes flick to his woman and back to the dipstick he was studying.

"You headin' for Jordan's Hole?" he asked at length in that same querulous tone. "Now? This hour? What you all want there?"

Val, dumbstruck by the audacity of his question, answered from sheer shock, "There's somebody there I know." After which, she recovered enough to inquire, "How far is it?"

There was that killing silence again, while he busied himself under the hood, adding oil and checking the battery. Finally he muttered in a tone that was a cross between insolence and jest, "Too far for you, m'am."

Valerie, after some lightning reflection, chose to answer the jest. "I've come this far, and I'm certainly not about to turn around now."

"Gets dark awful fast in them canyons. Not the best place to get caught at night with two young ones. Y' got no business there, m'am."

Val, having had enough of their exchange, smiled icily. "But I *have* business there. And I stopped being afraid of the dark a long time ago."

His eyes came at her like two metal spikes. But then he laughed, and Valerie would have opted for the spikes again.

"Are you finished there?" she asked brusquely.

"Just about." Then, as he straightened up and slammed the hood down, Gillian piped up,

"I wanna go to the bathroom."

"Me, too," Peter echoed.

Val groaned inwardly. "All right," she told them, turning a questioning glance at the man.

"Outhouses back of the buildin'," he said. He looked up at his wife, but she did not move. "I'll show you," he said, and as he led them through the littered rear yard, added, "Ol' lady's got a bum leg."

She may very well have, Valerie thought later. Still, in the interval while she was with the children, the woman had apparently left her rocker and come down the porch steps, for she was just climbing back when they returned.

Ready to roll once more, Val held a bill out to the man and waved off the change. He seemed not to notice, but leaning toward her spoke with a pressing earnestness. "Sure wish you'd change your mind. I'm thinkin' of those little kids. It's wild country in that canyon. Rockslides. Animals. Fellas shootin' at 'em all the time—"

"We'll be all right," Val said stiffly, cutting him off with a rev of the engine. Then they were away, picking up speed rapidly. Val was glad to see the last of the pair. In her rear-view mirror as she headed for the next bend, they stood frozen, watching her, their figures growing smaller and smaller until she lost them rounding the curve. Lost sight of them, that is, but curiously, not the chill of apprehension the man's unsubtle warnings had instilled. What was his purpose? With an effort, she tried shrugging the worry away, looking instead at the bright side. Without realizing it, Jake Jordan had at least disclosed to her that Jordan's Hole actually existed, something she had begun to doubt; in addition to assuring her that she was pointed in the right direction. As to his reasons for wanting her to stay out of the place, she hadn't a clue, but as she pressed on, for the first time since leaving home, she started taking Patty Linwood's situation seriously. Never mind that Patty said she was happy as a lark. That was weeks ago. And all this time she had been alone there with... what? Oh, God, she thought with a sudden stab of fear, what if she's— It was the closest she dared let her mind approach the unthinkable. But like a dog worrying a bone, her mind would not give up the gathering conviction that there was something in that canyon Jake Jordan did not want her to see.

Her mouth felt like flannel. In the seat behind her, Gillian whimpered, "Are we there yet?"

"Soon, darling. Open that package of cookies and nibble."

"It's getting dark," Peter quavered. "That man said—"

"That man was crazy, dear. Don't you worry about what he said. Besides, it's only dark down here between the canyon walls. Up there it's still light. See? It's not even sunset yet."

"But we're down here," he mumbled with the logic of a six year old.

"I know." She tried laughing. It came out tinnily. "I'm sure we're very close. I just have a f-feeling—"

She broke off sharply. From the car's front end came a hissing sound and at once a gush of steam clouding the trail ahead. Late to seize its meaning, she drove a few yards further, and abruptly the gush was a white wall blocking out the road. She braked instantly, switched off the motor, and jumping to the ground, hauled the children after her.

"Stand back—back now—I'm not sure what's happening—"

All the miles from New York there'd been no trouble with the Jaguar. And while she understood now the engine had overheated, she could not figure why. Or why *here!* And now! It seemed weird, coming on the heels of Jake's barely veiled warnings. Or did it?

Returning to the car after a few harried moments, she released the hood lever, then moved cautiously to the front to raise the hood, falling back from the searing steam. Waiting for it to dissipate, she glanced upward to where, thankfully, the skies still gleamed blue. But here it was dusk, and here the echoes of Jordan's warnings against entering the canyon took on new urgency.

"Not the best place to get caught at night with two young ones."

Those echoes, and the clammy new fears they stirred, were the chief reason Val bothered at all to look beneath the hood. For she knew perfectly well even if she could discover the cause of the trouble, there was virtually nothing she could do about it. But looking was doing *something!* And doing something was the therapy she needed to keep from losing her head. Or from admitting to herself how terrified she was.

In no time as she poked gingerly around the unfamiliar parts, her fingers became slippery with grease, and her hair falling forward a nuisance. She brushed it back impatiently, managing to streak her nose and cheeks liberally with the black stuff. She stopped long enough to bind it tightly to the back of her head, and secure it there with practiced fingers and a couple of long pins fished out of her handbag.

When she dived once again beneath the hood, she was only staving off that sickening moment when she must acknowledge that she was stranded for the night in this bleak canyon with two children who could scarcely be more petrified than herself.

Abruptly her searching fingers found the fanwheel—and

she knew at once what had happened. "The belt! It's gone—slipped off."

If that was all, if it had dropped out along the trail and she could find it, and if by hook or crook work it back on, if there was any water left in the radiator. If—if—! But she'd found the source of trouble. Now to find the belt. She kept feeling around on every ledge, every surface where it might have been caught. Nothing. On hands and knees she peered beneath the car, feeling the stony soil. Nothing.

She tried to calculate how far she'd driven—a matter of yards after the first sign of trouble. Bending low to the ground, she began searching her way back. The dusk was now purple gloom. At one point it was so dark, she had literally to grope along the ground. She dropped to her knees and spanned the rock-strewn trail with wide spreading hands, from side to side. From a boulder on her left, to a tree trunk on her right—a tree trunk?

Her breath died. Her heart went to mush ice. Something like a great chilling fist seized and wrenched her stomach.

The trunk had moved.

Chapter Five

SHE WAS ON her knees directly in front of it. Her head was scarcely a foot away. She saw now it was not alone; it had a twin.

A hushed groan scraped from her throat and she fell back, scrambling crablike across the trail. Inch by slow inch, her terrified stare rose up along the faded dungarees, and beyond, where denim ended and brown flesh glistened in the last fading light. Where a pair of arms bulging with muscles folded across a broad chest. The massive shoulders held her an unbelieving moment. Then she saw the gray eyes burning in the black-bearded face, and she forgot all the rest. Panic drove in. It was the silence that did it. The silence was thick and unnatural. *And where were the children?*

She strained listening above her own throbbing pulse-beat, but caught no sound, no voice. They had not been far off. Just behind her, playing beside the car—she thought.

Abruptly she cried out, "Where are the children?" and staggered to her feet.

"Good question, lady. Very good question," he said, his voice low and rumbly. His eyes, looking out from behind sooty-looking lashes, appraised her tall figure, rounded in all the right places. She decided to ignore the unwelcome assessment.

"Where are they?"she repeated when he showed no inclination to elaborate. "You know where they are."

"I just might," he conceded at length. "But anybody who lets two little kids wander loose until they're lost in this kind of country doesn't deserve to know. What were you doing crawling off on your hands and knees? Trying to abandon them or something?"

"*Abandon* them!" she gasped, and blind rage exploded. "If you want to know what happens in 'this kind of country,' I was hunting for a fanbelt which I begin to believe did *not* slip off by accident, but got helped off by a certain creep who runs a place called Jordan's. That's the kind of country this is!"

"Wait a minute, whoa, whoa! Who do you mean?"

"How many have you got like that?"

"You're talking about Jake Jordan?"

"That one."

"Come on. Jake wouldn't do a thing like that."

"Then there are two Jakes. This one deliberately did *some*thing to that belt to make it—"

"What in hell for?"

"You tell *me!* Tell me why he was so anxious to keep me out of this canyon—"

"Rubbish. It's in your head, lady. I know Jake. Know him well. He's a good guy."

"Sure he is. A pussycat! So maybe you can explain why my car which didn't give me an iota of trouble all the way from New York until I drove up to his place suddenly decided in the middle of the canyon he didn't want me to drive into to kick off its fanbelt—"

"Hey, hey, hey, I can't follow you, you're talking a blue streak." His eyes brimmed with amusement. "You're also talking nonsense. You think Jake's looking to antagonize people driving by? He needs every customer he can get, and he needs their good will. It's his living. Sure you're not making it all up?"

"That is the dumbest thing I ever heard. Are you calling me a liar?"

His elaborate shrug left the answer up to her. "You're on his side, of course," she told him, "because something tells me you know very well whatever it was he was trying to conceal at Jordan's Hole."

"Jordan's Hole!" She could see his eyes flicker and caught the significant drop in his tone. "What do *you* want at Jordan's Hole?"

Valerie's lips curled. "That's precisely the question *he* asked. Before he *suggested* I stay away."

"You're back to that now! Can we stick to the facts, lady?"

"Gladly! Fact one, Jake Jordan did not intimidate me one bit! And fact two, since you ask, neither do you. Now where are those children? *At once, please!*"

She'd moved up close enough to point a finger under his nose, a gesture that brought a twitch to his lips. He rocked back on his heels and scratched his head. Behind the beard, she suspected a thin smile. "I'm waiting," she fumed.

He leaned comfortably against the cliff wall, crossed one ankle over the other, and reached into a pocket for a pipe. He took his time knocking the bowl clean, and scrounged further for a pouch. When he'd finally begun tamping in tobacco, Valerie screamed, "Tell me what you've done with them!" The cliffs ping-ponged her voice from wall to wall, and he chuckled, listening.

"If this is my cue to say, 'You're beautiful when you're mad,' I pass, lady. The fella that made that one up never saw a mad woman with her jaw wagging, her face streaked with grease, her hair—forget it—and the voice of a peacock gargling gravel. Now I wonder how that ever got started?"

As he fished out a lighter and flicked it aflame, Valerie felt herself beginning to tremble uncontrollably. Suddenly everything blurred and the tears began to roll. She sobbed, "Wh-where are they, wh-what's happened to them?"

He paused only to pull at his pipe, his eyes shooting at

her through the orange glow. Then, with a curt "Follow me," he turned and strode off. Without another word, Valerie heeled. She was uncomfortably aware he had full control of the situation. And for the moment, of herself. Worse, even after she had the children safely back, she would still have to swallow his taunts and play meek and mild until he helped her get the car going again. *If* the wretch would agree.

He was so antagonistic, as if she had deliberately turned the children loose. Not that she could see much danger of their really getting lost. As they passed the disabled car, he brought the matter up as if it had been on his mind.

"Lucky for you I found them, lady. They could have gotten so lost, they'd turn up someday as skeletons. Only a mother with cotton batting for brains would let her kids wander through terrain like this—"

"I'm not their mother," she muttered pointlessly, but she chafed under his abuse.

"You're not?" That was good for a momentary silence from him. "Well, whatever you are, it was pretty dumb."

"I hardly see why. How could they get lost here anyway? All there is are sheer walls for as far as you can see."

"Are there?" he said. Moments later, he made such a sharp right turn she thought he would walk into the cliff face.

Valerie stared open-mouthed as he disappeared from view. Then she hurried after. Only when she stood directly before it did she discover the narrow cleft in the wall, the entrance to a side canyon that slanted back just enough to be virtually invisible to the casual traveler. A second offset, directly ahead, made the illusion complete.

The man turned, glancing over his shoulder. "Here's where I found them, looking almighty scared!"

He strode on, and she followed once again. When they entered the second opening, Valerie stopped short. The narrow entrance widened at once to a hitherto unseen trail. But at its mouth stood a Land Rover. "There," he said. And hurrying forward, Val saw Peter and Gillian fast asleep in the rear. Relief was so sharp, her tears spilled over again. "Thank God they're safe!"

"What did you think? I'd shot them?" In the near dark, his grin flashed white. But she suppressed her anger to thank him. "I can't tell you how relieved I am."

"You can stop your crying now and blow your nose! I've had enough hysterics for one day."

She ignored that. "I'll wake the children and take them—"

"Where?"

She hesitated, and he pressed it. "Where do you think you're going without that fanbelt you said you're missing?"

"Well, I—was wondering if you'd be so kind as to help me find one."

"Oh, sure, I run a fanbelt farm at the end of this trail. They grow right on the bushes. For Jaguars, our specialty. Lady, if that's what you need, Jake's your man, if he's got one."

"Him!"

"Sorry about that. Him. Meanwhile, you'd better spend the night with me."

Her head flung up. "With—*you!*"

"That's it, take it or leave it. And I've got an idea you'll take it."

Val never remembered wanting to slap a man so badly. Or worse, having to fight so hard restraining the impulse.

"Let's go," he said.

"Where?"

He slanted a look her way, his mouth twitching. And to her horror, he winked. "Jordan's Hole! It's what you wanted, isn't it?" Before she could answer, he opened the car door. "Get in." He moved around to the driver's side and got behind the wheel. Waiting, he began pulling on a heavy flannel shirt against the evening chill.

Val, still floundering about for some nonexistent alternative, finally gave it up and stepped primly in beside him. As the Land Rover took the hidden trail, she sat ramrod stiff, glaring through the windshield as far as his headlights permitted.

Even so, she caught the sound of the galloping horse seconds before it shot within the radius of the beams. Her breath died. There was a girl astride it, a goddess with flying red hair. Like the rest of the madness in this part of the world, she might have materialized out of the face of the cliff itself . . .

Chapter Six

THE MAN SAID NOTHING, but pulled over to the side and stopped. Valerie could feel him watching the girl intently, as the palomino came thundering along. The horse was very close when she saw the smile on the girl's face, and the way her eyes sought his.

"Hello—" she began, the horse skittering to a halt. But she broke off at once, the smile freezing. Her eyes, narrowing slowly, rested on Valerie. Slower still, her squared shoulders slumped, and Val noticed for the first time the bulging packsack suspended from them with some sort of a plastic container dangling from its strap.

"Yes, Ruby?" the man prompted when the silence threatened to stretch without end. "Did you finish?"

"Yes." It was the voice of a sullen child.

"Everything?"

Her brows pinched together. "Everything I had to."

"What's that supposed to mean?"

Her chin lifted, but her lips went to a thin line.

"Ruby, did you take the stuff?"

"Sure. Don't I always?"

"You know what I mean. Did you take all of it?"

She stared back a moment, mute. She was a vision,

nonetheless, Val thought, on that saddleless horse with her
snug faded jeans and yellow jersey that dipped much too
low in front. In the glow from the headbeams her eyes
showed green as jade—and angry. Her prominent breasts
rose and fell with her hard breathing, until impulsively
Valerie shot a glance at the man to see its effect. Abruptly
she was ashamed she'd even thought of it.

"I've asked you something Ruby," he reminded the girl,
though with considerably more patience than he'd extended
to Valerie earlier, she noted. "Did you take all of it?"

"No, I didn't!" she lashed back suddenly. "Why should
I?"

"Because I asked you to. Because I'm paying for it."

Her lower lip pushed out and she seemed close to tears.
The man waited, peering through the dimness at her packsack and the plastic container. "Hey! You've got only one
of the bottles!"

"I know it!"

"You'd better go back for the other. And for the rest of
the stuff!" There was annoyance in his tone now.

"I won't!" she retorted. "It's too dark. Ma'll be worried."

He laughed, quite brutally, Val thought. "It wasn't too
dark all those other times you stayed, Ruby. And I haven't
heard any complaints from your Ma yet. You're trying to
cop out of our bargain, right?"

Her hands tightened on the reins. Val thought she would
gallop off without answering, until she responded in a burst
of outrage, "It's not fair. Why do I have to look after her,
too? That wasn't in our bargain. Why must I take her laundry along with yours?"

"*Because you've got the water, girl!*" he roared all at
once. "And your ma's got the washing machine. And we've
got neither. And what kind of a dumb question is that from
a kid that's been around Jordan's Hole all her life?"

He waited for it to sink in before adding, quietly again,
"All right, now, turn that horse around like a good girl and
pick up the other things. Okay, Ruby? What are you waiting
for?"

The girl hesitated, her hands tightening again on the reins. Her eyes, Val was aware, had shifted to herself, and lingered there, even after she wheeled the palomino around. It was a bold look, an angry look. And suddenly she burst out again. "I reckon next you'll be tellin' me I got to look after hers, too, won't you?"

Val gasped, too stunned for more. But the man laughed, softly this time. "You would if I asked you, Ruby, wouldn't you?"

"Damned if I will, Nick McKenzie! Damned if I will!" And as she sent the horse into a furious gallop, Val fell back in the seat, her thoughts scattered like marbles.

Nick McKenzie! This man? This roughneck? This was who Patty thought she *loved?* Impossible. And yet . . . he was just the kind to attract the fluffy-headed little Pattys and Rubys of this world, lording it over them, as she'd just witnessed, as if he owned them! He was gazing after her now, his headbeams catching the last of her slender figure rounding a curve in the trail.

"She rides like the wind," he said, more to himself than to her. "Graceful as a willow. Beautiful!"

It shocked Val. The girl was too young and nubile, like Patty. And he was no kid. He was easily several years older than herself. Recalling the way he'd ordered the girl around and forced obedience from her, Val shrank within herself. What had he demanded of Patty? What hold did he have over her?

"Quite some girl," he murmured, starting the car again.

She could not resist sarcasm. "You're just the man to appreciate that, apparently."

He threw her another of his unholy winks. "When I stop appreciating that, I'm dead."

"That might be cause for celebration in some quarters."

He seemed to think that over. "Mm, I don't know. I'll have to ask my girls."

"What have you got there?" she scoffed. "A harem?"

"Just two. Care to make it three?" And before she could recover, "Isn't it time you told me what the devil you want at Jordan's Hole? After all, it's sort of my preserve. When I haul a woman in, I want to know where I stand with her."

She had to clench her fists in her lap. "I don't happen to find your sense of humor excruciating. As to where you stand with me, Mr. McKenzie? Exactly nowhere. Which is where you stood before you persuaded my cousin Patty Linwood to join you in—whatever you're carrying on back there in your so-called preserve!"

"Did you say *persuaded?*"

"You heard me. I've come to take that child home to her mother!"

"And welcome to her! *If* you can get her to leave—a skill I haven't quite mastered yet. Patty will not be enchanted!"

"I couldn't care less how enchanted she is. I wasn't exactly enchanted in having to trek all the way out here to get her, when I could have been having a fabulous time with my fiancé in New York."

"Oh? A fiancé, is it? Uh—where do those two fit in?" with a jerk of his head to the rear.

"The children?" She turned her head quickly, startled at having almost forgotten them. They were thankfully sleeping like lambs. "They're his. I thought they'd enjoy the trip."

"And he wouldn't?"

"He's a very busy man. In the middle of a lot of important work." She spoke tautly, resenting his prying.

"Then what have you missed at home? You might as well baby-sit his kids here as anyplace else!"

She was still casting about for a real crusher when he swung abruptly into a scene that made her forget everything else.

The trail had opened out magically, the cliff walls falling away as if sliced by a giant cleaver. The pale wash of a gibbous moon defined a clearing before them, and a clutch of huts in a random semicircle. Clumps of growth and a scattering of boulders dotted the open area, while back of it all rose a dark and brush-covered slope.

From the windows and doors of two of the small cabins, a thin light wavered, as from candles. But Valerie's attention was immediately distracted as Ruby, still astride her horse, came clip-clopping to meet them. Before McKenzie had even shut off the motor, she snapped, "*That* was a waste of time! The princess won't let me take her things! I could have been home by now."

The princess, Val thought. Yes, that would be Patty, all right. And in fact, as she watched from the darkness of the car, there she stood, framed in one of the lighted doorways. Valerie's mood was such by now that when McKenzie roared "Patty!" she herself would have gladly given the girl a shaking, by way of greeting.

"What the devil's all the fuss?" he added, stepping from the car. "I sent Ruby back to get your things so her mother can launder them!"

"Well, you needn't have bothered, Nicky dear. She's not going to do *me* any favors! I am quite capable of laundering my own—"

"Without water? You little idiot!"

"Ni-ick!" Patty cried, wounded. In a second, Val knew, if nobody stopped her she would turn on the tears, an art she had mastered at the age of twelve, and with such finesse it never failed to bring any man within the range of her voice running with shoulder extended. As it would bring *that* one, too, for all his bluster! Valerie relaxed, enjoying the spectacle, until abruptly the scenario changed.

"*Patty!*" His voice dropped several decibels. "I'll give you two seconds flat to get your things together and hand them over!"

"N-Ni-ick—"

"*Move!*" he shouted. "*On the double!*"

Patty turned and went inside, if not exactly on the double, at least without another word. Valerie thought she had just witnessed history. Nobody ever before had gotten that kind of action from the girl on anything she hadn't wanted to do!

While they were waiting for her to reappear, something

happened that was to baffle and nag at her for some time to come. Nick McKenzie walked back to where Ruby sat her horse close by the car. Val clearly saw him reach up and pat her hand. "Sorry, honey, for all the trouble," he murmured.

She watched from the corner of her eye as the girl's face lit slowly. "It's all right, Nick," she said. "I—I don't really mind her. It's just that everything's changed since she came."

"No. No it hasn't, Ruby. It's the same as ever. And I have a very large notion she'll be gone before long. There's this very determined lady from New York"— with a jerk of his head in her direction, so that Val knew she was meant to hear—"who seems to think she can handle her."

The girl smiled broadly now. In the moonlight, her eyes seemed to glisten as Nick turned and strode back to where Patty had emerged at last, with what must have been everything she owned that was washable. Nick's voice went sharp again. "You're not going to hand it to her that way!"

"Why not?"

"Get it together in a sack. I gave you a sack. What did you do with it?"

"How should I know? At home the maid handles those things—".

"You're not at home, girl—to my everlasting regret! And Ruby is not your maid, just because her mother handles the washing. And don't you ever forget that!"

This time as Patty turned back for the sack, Val knew from the droop of her head that she was crying—for real. At least, she thought, it won't be any big deal to get her to leave. She must know she's not welcome here. Thank heaven we'll be gone from this place as soon as we find that fanbelt. Tomorrow, some time.

But there was still the night to live through.

And that was the night of the music . . .

Chapter Seven

VALERIE FELT BONE-WEARY. The children, thoroughly exhausted by the long hot day, never stirred after Ruby galloped off again, her packsack fatter for Patty's laundry, and two more plastic bottles dangling from the straps.

Valerie wondered about all that baffling talk about water, or the lack of it. She would have liked nothing so much as a steaming tub and a good bed to stretch out on. But she knew that was hardly on the agenda for this night. And first, there was Patty to be faced. Val saw her cousin sulking alone watching Nick McKenzie gazing after Ruby until she was lost from view. For all his sternness with the girl on the trail, he certainly seemed attracted to her, Val thought. Her age, about the same as Patty's, she guessed, would hardly deter a man like him, who blithely acknowledged he'd be dead when he could no longer appreciate charms like hers!

Val was in a prickly mood when he approached her again.

"Kids still asleep? Good. They might as well stay there. I've got some blankets, right here. It gets cold at night."

He felt around and hauled out a couple of rolls, which he shook out and tucked around Peter and Gillian. The children never moved. "Now for Patty," he said. "Come ahead."

Valerie got down from the car and followed, though she loathed his way of snapping orders. Still she had no choice, and much as she hated admitting it, he had spared her and the children a terrifying night alone in the middle of nowhere.

Patty had turned her back dramatically. Val thought the move was meant to bring Nick crawling with apologies for his callousness. When he called out across the clearing, "Hey, Patty, you've got company," the girl turned slowly, as if expecting a ruse to work his way back into her good graces.

She saw Valerie with him, but recognition seemed slow in coming, which was not surprising considering her cousin's condition—rumpled, dust-stained, and grease-streaked from the day's ordeal. Val's tight bun was the only thing that had remained in place and it was far from flattering. She would have died rather than let Barry see her like that. As for McKenzie's uncomplimentary remarks, he was hardly the best-groomed man *she'd* ever seen, either!

"Company—wh-who?" Patty began peering uncertainly.

"I'd give you three guesses, but you'd drag it out using them all!"

"You're still mad, Nick, aren't you?"

"Mad enough to be damn glad you're going home tomorrow!"

"Who said—? Oh—" Here for the first time she recognized her cousin. "Valerie! Damn! What are *you* doing here? Why did you come? I've been so happy!"

Val sighed. "Then you're the only one who *has* been, Patty! And I didn't come because I wanted to. I'd much rather have been at home with Barry!"

"You should have stayed there! I'm getting along beautifully!"

"Your mother isn't. Don't you ever consider anyone except yourself? You didn't even phone and I saw a telephone emblem on the Jordans' front porch!"

The girl clammed up so abruptly, Valerie glanced to Nick for some clue. He was standing with his arms folded, obviously running out of patience.

At length, clearly annoyed, he said, "Patty, you can finish your battle in the morning. I've about had it. Wasted a whole afternoon when I could have been working before the sun went down." At what, Valerie wondered briefly, recalling that he had apparently been on his way out of the hidden trail when things began to happen. But he'd said nothing to her about work. "Your cousin had a tough grind, and she needs a bit of rest, I'd say."

Val nodded. "Thank you, I'd like that, Mr. McKenzie."

"Nick, to you, too. Okay, Patty, stop your grouching and take her around to the water drums so she can wash up." And to Val, he added quickly, "Don't waste any. Every drop has to be hauled in. Ruby brings the drinking water, her dad trucks in the drums. There's never enough, especially the way the princess here thinks it's for her own special accommodation!"

"That's not fair! Ruby uses her share, cleaning your cabin," Patty snapped.

"And yours, too. Which somehow gets messier than I'd have thought possible with one girl! Now just shut up and do what I told you. You'll have to lend your cousin what she needs. Her bags are still out at the trail."

"Why didn't you bring them?"

"Because you'll all be leaving tomorrow. Just as quickly as I can get her car fixed!"

Patty moaned, "Val, why did you come? When I've never been so happy before in all my life?"

"That has a familiar ring," Valerie murmured. "Now where do I wash up?"

Patty turned reluctantly, and as Valerie started to follow, her eyes grazed Nick's, catching a glint of humor. Without thinking, she returned it. But when he smiled, with a sudden flash of white in that black-bearded face, she turned quickly and hurried after Patty. Had she not seen him earlier in a stronger light, she might have thought him almost . . . attractive.

At the rear of her cabin, where Patty led her, dawdling, sat a couple of lidded drums beside a metal basin. Patty pointed to an old tin ladle. "There! You bail it out with that and you've got to empty the basin when you're finished. *He* says! Though I don't know why Ruby can't do that. She gets paid for it, and she's here every day."

"You heard him, the girl's not your personal maid."

"Oh, he always puts on an act like that when anyone's around. Just to hide the truth."

"What truth?" Val asked idly, carefully measuring wash water into the basin. The night air had grown chill, but she stripped to the waist and using a large bar of soap and a cloth Patty handed her from a shrub where it had been drying, she began scrubbing and rinsing as best she could under the primitive conditions.

"The truth," Patty announced, "is that Nick's in love with me. He'll deny it every time, but it doesn't change things any."

"Really!" Val started rubbing down with a thick towel Patty provided. "You mean he's admitted it when you were alone? He's said, 'I love you, Patty'?"

"Don't be so picky-picky, Val! Did Barry have to tell you in so many words before you knew it?"

She smiled. "He didn't have to, but he did. Often."

"So? What did that prove? Considering—"

Val flared. "Just leave the considering to *me*, Patty! As for your Nick, you don't know a darned thing about him, least of all that he's in love with you!" Suddenly her mind was alive with questions. "Who is he? *What* is he? What's this crazy place all about?" she cried. "And most of all, why *didn't* you phone when you could have? You didn't answer me before."

"With Nick standing there? He'd only say I was imagining. Or lying. But I wouldn't go near that place. Those people—Jake, especially. He hates me, and she does, too.

Sure, they were okay when the girls were still with me. But when I dropped in later and mentioned I was staying on, I thought they'd—kill me! You should have heard Millie! She said"—mimicking the old woman's twang—"'young girls got no business alone with grown men!' I asked her, 'How come it's all right for Ruby?'"

"Ruby!"

"Sure. She's their own daughter—"

"She certainly doesn't look it!"

"Well, all right, she's pretty," Patty conceded reluctantly. "But she's always hanging around Nick. And her mother said, 'Ruby's got work to do for a livin' and besides it ain't none of your business!'"

"Which it isn't."

"I think it is," Patty retorted, bridling. "Especially if they're going to glare threats at me."

Val hesitated, unwilling to confide her own experience, but anxious to know more. "*Did* they threaten you?"

Patty's mouth went grim. "I don't know what Nick would call it. He laughed like crazy when I told him. But I know what I saw. And when I told Mrs. Jordan, 'Then my staying here is none of your business, either,' I saw the look she and her husband passed each other. And I also saw that rifle he's never without. Believe it, he made sure I did."

"The rifle? Yes, I saw it, too. But what's that got to do with anything?"

"Val, I'm not stupid. All the time I was over there, he was handling it, cleaning it, fondling it, squinting through the sites. And I say it was no mere chance that most of that squinting was in my direction. If that's not threatening, I don't know what else to call it."

"I'd call it overreacting, Patty. Granted he's not my favorite person either, but lots of men carry rifles in hunting country. You're just not used to seeing it."

"Have it your way." Patty shrugged. "That's just what Nick said when I told him. I thought he'd split his sides laughing. But I *expected* that. You don't think he's going to side with me and offend those people, do you?"

"Why not? What if he walked in there and read them
the riot act?"

"Ha! What if they refused to sell him any water? There's
no place else to get it and he couldn't stay here without it.
Besides, they own the land. But mostly it's the water.
Without the water, this place is dead!"

"Well, what is it *now*, for heaven's sake?" Val laughed.
She broke off at a sound beyond the cabin. From somewhere in the shadows, Nick called, "Hurry it up, girls. I've
got a meal cooking!"

Val clutched the towel around her, but almost at once
his steps receded.

"Does he always creep up on you in the dark?" she
whispered nervously.

Patty sniffed. "Of course not. He respects me too much.
It's why he won't touch me!"

Val smothered a laugh, her hands busy at the pins in her
hair. "Comb?"

"Hairbrush," Patty said and slipped around to the cabin
door to get one. When she returned, Val was shaking her
long black hair free. Patty gazed at it in the moonlight.

"I should never have cut my hair for the trip," she said
mournfully. "The girls thought it would be easier to care
for. I wish I'd left it the way it was. Ruby's is—too much."

Val smiled, brushing out the day's dust vigorously.
"Short suits you."

"Men go for long."

"Don't you ever think of anything except men?"

"What else is there?" She turned and started off, gloom-
ily, Val following again. At the cabin door she took the
brush from Val's hand and chucked it inside without even
looking.

"Something smells fabulous!" Val breathed.

"He cooks, too," Patty said. "But even if he didn't, I'd
still adore him!"

Walking across the clearing to the farthest cabin, Valerie

paused to peer into the Land Rover. The children slept like angels. She tucked the blankets in closer, then headed for Nick's door.

Inside, the glow from several candles was warmly golden. He had set up a rough board table in the center of the room, and spread it with a collection of tin plates and utensils like nothing Val had seen before. The coffee mugs were tin as well, and the cabin was redolent with the aroma of a fresh brew. Everything about it seemed old, very old, and her curiosity dug deep. But her hunger dug even deeper and she was not about to delay the meal with questions.

At a small camp stove mounted on an upended crate in a corner, Nick stood, his back to them, stirring the contents of a large iron kettle. Valerie's mouth watered, even as she realized this was something else she would be indebted to him for. But he would be even more indebted to her for relieving him of Patty, so perhaps they were even.

"You can find your places," he said without turning. "This stew's been simmering all day. If the kids wake up there's enough for them."

"They won't," Val assured him. "They sleep like logs."

He turned to reach for a potholder. It had fallen to the dirt floor and gotten kicked a distance off. "Hand me that, Patty, will you—" he began, and abruptly broke off. His glance had stopped at Val and held. For a time too scant to measure, his eyes registered . . . something. Patty, scooping up the potholder, held it out to him. He did not move.

"Well, here!" she said petulantly. He took it and turned back wordless. When he finally spoke he said nothing monumental, only, "I see you got cleaned up. Hope you didn't run the water drum dry!"

"I used two and two-thirds scoopfuls," Val answered. "It was only surface dirt."

"Considering the change," he mumbled over the stew kettle, "it was a pretty deep surface."

"Oh, let's sit down!" Patty exploded.

"What's holding you?" Nick growled back, carrying the bubbling iron pot to the table. Val thought she'd never smelled anything so good. But Patty, in the ugliest of moods, snapped, "Don't tell me you've gone and fixed another of those ragouts à la Jordan, Nick?"

"Watch it, kid," he muttered, reaching for Valerie's bowl to fill. "You've been sent to your cabin for less reason than that!"

"Stop treating me like a child, Nick," the girl said, her voice going scratchy, "just because Valerie's here to impress!"

"I'll treat you like a child as long as you act like one!" He was completely composed. "And for reasons that totally elude me, you always act like one when there are other people present—other women, I might point out."

"That's not true!"

"If you're going to mess up this meal with a battle royal, Princess, you can take your exalted majesty to hell back to your bunkhouse. And let *us* eat in peace!"

Patty looked close to tears. "You'd like nothing better, wouldn't you, Nick? You always put on this act for company. Even when it's only that kid Ruby—"

"*Get lost!*" he roared, his eyes blazing. "You're spoiled so rotten I'm surprised your mother even *wants* you back! I should think she'd be singing hallelujah!"

Patty's chair crashed to the floor as she sprang up. "It's all you need, Nick—a new woman on the scene, and you're mean as dirt. But as soon as we're alone, it's a different story."

"Great imagination, kid! Now make yourself scarce before I forget everything I ever learned about how to treat girls!"

Choking back her tears, Patty fled from the cabin. Valerie, forgetting her hunger, half rose to follow.

"Where are *you* going?"

"To see that she's all right."

"Sit down. You're not going anyplace."

"Don't start that lord and master act on *me*, Nick, really."

"I will if the situation demands. Sit down and eat." He shoved her steaming bowl in front of her and filled his own.

Valerie sat. The aroma was too much. And Patty *had* been everything he'd said. Spoiled rotten—and absurdly jealous of *her!* She reached for her fork.

"Use your spoon," Nick growled. "It's soupy."

"I see." Tentatively she dipped her spoon and found a chunk of beef. She lifted it delicately to her mouth. Patty's reference to ragout à la Jordan had put her off a little. But the gravy, the seasonings, the meat were superb. She raised her eyes, feeling his upon her.

"Well?" It was almost a challenge.

"Good."

"That's all?"

"Very good."

"Damned right!" He took a spoonful, chewed, and swallowed. "Ragout à la Jordan, my sainted aunt!" he mumbled. "*Anything* à la Jordan brings out the worst in that kid, and perhaps you have some idea how 'worst' worst can get!"

Valerie changed the subject, seeing no reason for disloyalty to family. "What *is* this recipe?"

He smiled. "It's Millie Jordan's all right, with herbs you never heard about. A family recipe that dates back to the early mining-camp days here."

"Mining camp! Here?"

"Here. Or to be accurate, some miles south of here. One of the wildest silver booms in the territory. But that goes back a hundred years. Nothing but a ghost town there now."

"But here, what is this?"

"Here, ha! Jordan's Hole. This place wouldn't have existed at all except for one of Jake Jordan's very stubborn forebears. Up there where the store is, and those outbuildings, where they carry on their flourishing car-sabotaging industry—" He grinned, and Val nearly choked on her rage.

"I know what they did, in spite of your questionable loyalty."

"You and your cousin both. You're neurotic about those people. Do you want to hear about Jordan's Hole?"

For a second, she didn't care if she heard or not. But curiosity won out. She nodded.

"Well, there at the site of the store, was, and is, the only water for miles around the area. Jake's great-great-grandfather owned acres and acres with all the springs in sight. He got rich selling and delivering water to the mines—at four cents a gallon in those days—because down that way they didn't have a drop! All they had was silver. Then he wanted to get richer. He had some notion there was a vein under his land up here. And he figured to start his own operations. He had the machinery hauled in, expensively, built these cabins for the work crews, and set the men to digging, and digging; but all he ever got out of it except for a thin trace of silver was a hole in the ground. Stubborn old guy, he was. Used up most of his fortune, even after engineers and assayers assured him he was wasting his time. The place got to be a local joke. Jordan's Hole. But nobody laughed too loud. At least not where old Jordan was likely to hear. Because he still had the water, and without him and it they were through. Of course, as it happened, pretty soon they were through anyway. Their own veins ran out, and the main mine collapsed and the silver boom was finished around here. And so, as it turned out, was Jordan's water business. There's nothing left but what you saw. Travel being what it is these days, who needs Jake's water all that much?"

"You do." Valerie smiled.

"Oh, sure. I couldn't stay on without it, could I?"

"Of course not. And so"—she was beginning to enjoy herself—"you don't want to believe they're anything but darlings, that awful couple. You wouldn't *let* yourself believe they had anything to do with the Jag breaking down. Or even if you conceded a bare possibility, obviously you would not express it in front of their daughter Ruby, who would probably carry it right straight back to them. The way she glared at me on the trail!"

"Now, *hey!*"

She wouldn't have believed the instant change in him. His eyes smoldered. And the spoon he held came thrusting at her like a spear.

"You leave that girl out of this discussion. Or any other, as long as you're around!"

"Which won't be long to trouble either you—*or* that *child!*"

Her emphasis was not lost on him. His mouth twisted in a scornful smile. "Just to sort things out," he muttered, "she's nineteen. You look after your 'child.' I'll look after mine! Right? Now eat."

Her gorge rose. "I've had enough. Thank you."

"Good. I'll show you your bed."

Her bed . . . ? The thing had a funny sound. "I'll check the children and go to sleep with Patty."

"I've checked the children, and will again. And it would take you until morning to clear off the clutter in Patty's place so you can even *find* another bunk. You'll sleep here. In mine!"

Val's lips fell open. She couldn't have heard that right. He caught the thick silence and met her eyes head on. "I'll take one of the other cabins," she murmured.

"Help yourself, if you want to share it with a hundred years of cobwebs, rats, insects—"

She swallowed hard. "I'll—sleep with the children—"

"You'll do as I say! You're almost as bad as Patty. Must be a family trait—argue, argue, argue—"

"*I will not sleep in this cabin with you!*" she burst out all at once.

He stared at her, then laughed infuriatingly. "And I will not sleep in this cabin with you either, honey!" He said softly. "I'm afraid you presume a bit much!"

Val's cheeks burned. She felt exactly the sort of fool he'd set out to make of her.

"I'll take a blanket roll under the stars," he added. "And it won't be the first time. Besides, I've got work to do."

She refrained from asking what kind of work he would do in the dead of night in a blanket roll under the stars. It chilled her even to think about it. Silently she helped him clear the table, then dry the dishes with paper towels as he washed them in water that had been heating while they ate.

She found nothing amusing when he said, "At least you earn your keep here, which is more than I've been able to say about the princess!"

She watched from the corner of her eye as he prepared his bunkbed for her, hoisted a blanket roll from another, and turned to leave. Two more things he took with him that aroused her curiosity—an attaché case that seemed grotesquely out of place in this setting and an electric lantern.

"G'night," he told her, "It's all yours." And as a last gesture he removed an old flannel robe from a hook and tossed it to her. "For company, if you get lonely."

She heard his low, mocking laughter long after he'd closed the door between them.

The moment he was gone, she replaced his robe on its hook. Chilly though the night was, it would have had to be Antarctica before she'd put that thing on!

She snuffed the candles and crept into his bunkbed. She was greeted instantly with his tobacco odor which pervaded the blanket, though not unpleasantly. His pillow had a man-smell to it. He hadn't given her a fresh one. It was, after all, not the Waldorf. Still, it was better than the open trail. She was grateful enough. Her thoughts rambled, wondering how quickly they might get started in the morning. Certainly if Jordan's had no fanbelt for the Jaguar, she was quite sure Jake would knock himself out finding one for her once he learned she'd actually made it to Jordan's Hole after all. Valerie still hadn't the faintest idea why he'd tried to keep her from finding the place, but surely that seemed his intention. She no longer had the slightest doubt, for all Nick's hee-hawing, that he had loosened, or even slit the belt, just to keep her from going very far. If she'd broken down sooner, she'd have been forced to return to him for help, hopefully harassed enough by that time to leave the area and never return.

And what of this business that Patty referred to, the thing about the rifle? Until this moment, alone in the dark, she had wanted very much to laugh that off. Yet, they were such a terrible couple. Would Jake resort to a threat like that, empty perhaps, but a threat all the same? And if so, why?

Her mind kept going in circles, until mercifully sleep began hazing over. She sighed, and was sinking deeper and deeper into the warm . . . when the music trickled into her consciousness . . . note upon thin note . . . plaintive as a nightbird calling . . . with a sweetness that tugged her awake . . .

She sat up listening, knowing now she was not dreaming. The music was close at hand, too. She rose and glided to the single screened window. She could see nothing. She stared into the moonglow, straining to follow the direction of the sound. But it seemed to be everywhere, rising and falling, surging and fading. The night air, after the warm bed, seized and shook her.

Without thinking, too intent on the melody, she reached to the hook and found the flannel robe. Still listening, still baffled, she worked her arms into the voluminous sleeves. She gathered up the folds and secured them tightly around her with the trailing cord. Miles too-large, the robe dragged on the floor. She hiked it up and concentrated again on the music through the square of window that afforded such a limited view.

The dulcet strains made magic. She had never heard their like. They flowed with the haunting sweetness of water on pebbles in a sunlit forest pool.

Cautiously, at last she opened the door, wincing as it creaked. She moved out beneath such stars as she had never known existed. Their radiance lay soft on the cabin roofs, and on the Land Rover where the children slept, and on the barren space between. She moved to its center, the better to pinpoint the melody's source . . .

And abruptly it sliced off clean. In the silence that rushed in to fill the gap, she stood frozen, sensing eyes upon her.

From the growth skirting the clearing well behind her, she heard, *"Room Service. You called?"*

Chapter Eight

SHE LONGED TO RUN. She could not move, not even turn in the direction from which he approached with leisurely steps. She knew at last what a cat felt like, surprised beneath the canary cage with a mouthful of yellow feathers.

"You want the idiot on the terrace with the fluegelhorn ejected at once, madam? The management will see to it."

"Don't be silly," she muttered. "I—only came to check the children."

"I was just over there. Peter woke up and said to kiss you good night!"

"Brilliant sense of humor that kid has."

"That's about what I told him. Have I and my little fipple flute disturbed you?"

"Fipple flute!" She glanced down at the instrument he held. "They called mine a recorder in kindergarten."

"That, and you, have come a long way since. But if it makes you happy, a recorder then."

"What on earth are you playing to the moon for?"

"Can you think of a better audience? And it's not play, it's work."

"In the middle of the night?"

"You've seen what goes on here in the daytime. Though

I'll admit it's only been like this since Patty came barging in here with her friends and hired herself on as my private hair shirt! If I'm to get anything done at all, it's got to be at night. And when we have an overflow of guests so that I have to give up my cabin—"

"I'll be out of here tomorrow. As soon as you can run down a fanbelt. You'll try, I'm sure? Early?"

"My pleasure."

And mine, too, Val thought. But curiosity prompted a last question. "What on earth are you working at, anyway?"

"Music."

"I know that," she said impatiently.

"Writing it."

She suppressed an acid laugh. "If you *really* wrote that, what are you doing stuck out here in never-never land, instead of someplace where it can do you some good?"

"Meaning, I suppose, an overpriced city apartment? I tried that while I was still in school. Juilliard, in fact—in your own home town."

"Oh?" She could not keep the respect from her voice.

"Yes. With all the rumble of traffic below. Jets overhead. TVs screeching. Radios blaring. And worst of all, the human voice, forever drowning out—"

"Inspiration!" She said it tauntingly. She thought she knew the type. Never short of excuses for their own failures.

"I was going to say, drowning out a listening ear, if that means anything."

"I'll remember that." She yawned.

"Do. And you might try it sometime instead of forever interrupting. Another family trait."

"Which you won't be troubled with after tomorrow, hopefully."

"Amen. Shall I escort you back?"

She had said nothing about leaving, and his pointed dismissal flustered and humiliated her. "Thank you, I can find my way." She swung around while saying it, only to trip over the robe dragging at her feet, and promptly pitched forward. But she never hit the ground. His arm stopped her, and held her, even after she said, "Thanks. I'm all right now."

She wasn't. Her ankle had twisted sharply.

"Then why are you scrunching up in pain?"

"Who's in pain?"

"O-*kay!*" He released her at once. She hoisted the robe, took a step, and sank to the ground, groaning.

"Hell, more trouble!" He sounded annoyed rather than concerned about her as he bent to scoop her off the ground.

"I can limp back. I just wasn't prepared. It's no sprain, I'm sure."

"This is easier on my nerves," he grumbled, striding with her to the cabin as if she were a ten year old.

"Let me see it," he said when he had deposited her on the bunk and lighted a candle. Val winced when he touched it. "It's swelling but I doubt it's a fracture," he concluded. At the water supply, he dipped and wrung out a towel. Returning, he wrapped it around the bulging ankle. It felt icy cold and good. Valerie sighed. "Th-thanks, I'm sorry for the trouble."

He hesitated. In the wavering candle light she thought he smiled. "Women are always trouble," he said. Unexpectedly, his hand reached out to her, brushing her cheek, then lost itself a moment in her hair, lingering there. "It's— it's real," he murmured.

The sudden racing of her blood, the tremulous excitement filling her throat startled her. It made of her swift retort, "What were you expecting, feathers?" a foolish, fluttery whisper, and brought his eyes to hers, laughing all at once, knowing as he must have known that he had done this to her. The tip of her tongue circled her parted lips in a frantic gesture, serving only to moisten them until they gleamed in the candle's thin glow. She knew the precise moment his gaze fell to them, and hung there, deliberating. Another instant and she would put an end to it. She would rise up, ankle or no ankle, and ask him what he thought he might be doing. Let his face come an inch closer, and she would give him something to think about! Her clenched hand was ready and waiting, her mind spilling over with all the things she would do to him, say to him . . . and her breath failed. Her head fell back, her eyes shut, feeling his mouth covering hers, knowing he was finding it soft, unresisting, even surrendering, a little. She felt the gasp in her throat as his arm shot around behind her, drawing her body to his, suddenly avid. She struggled halfway erect as avidity threatened to erupt into a passion that frightened her. She felt him straining against her, forcing her slowly back down again upon the bunk, his mouth never relenting, not for a dizzying moment, crushing her lips beneath his like sweet ripe grapes.

Then he released her, so abruptly that it sent her scrambling about in her head for the remnants of her anger, and all the things she was "going to do to him."

"Why did you *do* that?" she gasped at length, knowing how lame it sounded.

His dry laugh was no answer. "You wanted that, didn't you?" he murmured, twisting the thing to appear of her making. "You did. Admit it. You wanted it a little. More than a little?"

And before she could bring together the appropriate tongue-lashing, he whispered, "Get some sleep," and was gone.

Sleep . . . after *that?* Her hand kept wandering to her mouth where his had clung. Belief hung suspended in a realm where only dreams abide, the sort that one knows did not, *could not* have happened. It was not possible that she had seen what was coming, known she could have stopped it, and still let it happen. And—all *right*—found nothing reprehensible in it. Found instead a momentary surge of pleasure. It didn't last long enough to count, of course. A fraction of an instant. Less. But for that fraction, and this was what stunned her, she had not shrunk from it. She had not shriveled with distaste. She had—liked it, in a way she hadn't liked any man's kiss except Barry's.

What troubled her now above all, invading her restless sleep, was that Nick McKenzie knew all this about her.

Knew beyond a doubt what had happened to her there in his arms. And would make pretty darned sure she knew that he knew. The arrogant, self-satisfied . . . ugh!

She awoke to a rat-ta-tat of hoofbeats, and the dawn light at the cabin window. Suddenly, a flashing image of the red-haired girl streaked past . . . "like the wind, graceful as a willow." The words whipped back into her consciousness and sank there like lead. Nick's heated defense of the girl lay there from the night before. She had felt severely chastised, out in the cold, like Patty. "So who cares?" She shrugged, sitting up in the chill air.

Abruptly she dodged an answer. Breathing in deeply, she felt her lips, recalling with an insane nostalgia the way it had been, every quivering detail that led to his possession of them.

She was crazy to have let it happen. Now there would be that humiliation to deal with, as if the day didn't promise difficulty enough. She sighed and felt her ankle; the swelling had reduced. Stepping down cautiously, she found the pain to be tolerable. At least, she thought, this little bit of ointment in my jar of flies!

She struggled from bed, limping to the wash basin while she gathered her forces. She must see the children first. Then Barry must be called. He'd be frantic if he didn't hear from them soon. There was the phone at Jordan's, though she'd rather not have to resort to that. As soon as the car was in order, and Patty in it—straitjacketed if necessary—they'd be on their way.

After a superficial wash-up at Nick's bucket, she dressed and walked gingerly into the early sunlight. A cloudless blue sky greeted her, and a cathedral-like hush. She did not see Ruby anywhere and could not imagine what had brought the girl so early. But she saw Peter and Gillian sitting cross-legged Indian fashion on the ground, tin plates on their laps from which they were scraping the last of some breakfast Nick had evidently prepared for them, which was decent of him, she did not deny.

She walked over to the children whose only greeting was, "We're finished, can we play?"

"What, no morning kiss for me?"

Gillian obliged readily, but Peter merely announced, "He gave us eggs and bacon."

"*He* is Mr. McKenzie."

"He said to call him Nick. And he said we can play anyplace down here but not to go up there." Peter pointed toward the slope where halfway up Valerie could see a mound of rotting timbers overgrown with vegetation. "Nick said there's a hole there and we mustn't go that way."

The hole, yes, Val recalled. Jordan's Hole. The opening of the aborted mine. "Well, you stay clear of that. That's very, very dangerous."

"Aw, we know," Peter said impatiently and the two raced off together just as Patty appeared in her door. Valerie went to greet her.

"It's beautiful here!"

"I know. That's why I'm not leaving."

"We'll talk about that when the car's ready!"

"We'll talk about nothing, Val! You're wasting your time."

"You're in a lovely mood again, I must say. I hoped you'd sleep it off."

"I might have, but did *you* enjoy being awakened before dawn by that pushy kid galloping in like the U.S. Cavalry with those stupid water bottles? She doesn't even give him a chance to wake up!"

"He was awake."

"He—how do you know?" She sounded aghast. "Say, where did *you* sleep last night, Val?"

"Oh, come on, you're absurd. Go wash up. I'm starved for some breakfast."

"I want to know." The girl seemed dead serious.

"All right, then. In his cabin. In his bed, in fact! He tucked me in. Does that satisfy you?"

Patty swallowed a couple of times as if she might burst into tears. "I never thought *you*—Val—"

"Oh, you little dumdum!" Valerie groaned. "I slept alone. I'm not quite the pushover you'd like to be, Patty dear—" She broke off, sensing that she was speaking rather more stridently than necessary. Resuming on a quieter note, she added, "Besides, you *know* I'm crazy in love with Barry. That should relieve your mind."

The children came racing from behind the cabin, startling Patty, who had never met them, and giving Val a chance to change the subject.

"This is Gillian and Peter, Barry's youngsters."

"Oh, they're cute," Patty said as they raced straight off again. "Val—you're really going to marry Barry, finally?"

"As quickly as his new agency gets off the ground. He's been frightfully busy. It's why I brought the children with me, and it's a chance to get to know each other. I really adore them. They're no trouble at all. Which is something their mother apparently never took the time to find out."

Patty tossed a towel across her shoulder and headed back to the water basin. "Maybe she was too busy keeping Barry in line!"

"Hey-y! That's a nasty thing to say!" Val protested.

"It was a nasty divorce, wasn't it?"

Val's anger sent her spinning around and off in search of Nick. The sooner they were away, the better. She'd have given almost anything, nonetheless, not to have to face him after that incredible happening in the night, and her swift pace slowed markedly, reflecting on it. It was not going to be easy. He was not going to let her forget it. But she'd about had it with Patty, even acknowledging her young cousin's frustration had her flailing at everybody in all directions. She'd probably be a horror on the return trip, but Val was sure the first male who smiled at her again—and a lot had—would take care of that.

Up ahead she saw Ruby's horse grazing at the edge of the clearing. Logically, Nick would be somewhere around there, where apparently he had spent the night.

She came upon them suddenly, together on the ground. They had not heard her as she rounded the farthest cabin, though she'd made no effort to muffle her steps on the stony soil. They sat close, Nick leaning over a flat rock, writing. His back was turned to her, and for a devastating instant, the sight of his wide shoulders played wickedly on her consciousness. The weight of them, the warmth of his body, the hardness of his arms, all ricocheted sensuously from the night before, and appalled her. With enormous effort, she dragged her mind back to the cool, crisp morning. To reality. Back from all that nighttime silliness, to dwell momentarily on the girl. The girl was singing. Softly, in a small thin voice. Her face was lifted to the early light, her eyes shut beneath that abundance of red-gold hair. Her knees were drawn up, her hands clasped around them, while she swayed to the rhythm of her tune.

Valerie watched spellbound. There was something about this girl. A thing she had felt with that first sight of her astride the palomino in the dusk. She was different. She had something that Patty lacked, would never have! An earnestness, perhaps. Of course, it was plain she also worshipped Nick, just as it was becoming clearer all the time that Nick was not exactly indifferent to her. This business of the girl working for him had a sort of phony ring, though it served very well to bring the two together each day perhaps. But certainly, Val thought with sudden distaste, there was more between those two than a sack of laundry!

She was young. Nineteen, he'd said. But nineteen in the wilds was a very different affair from nineteen in the sophisticated city. She was tall, built like a mountain woman . . . built for men, for bearing children. Yes, a man like Nick, wearing his virility out in the open where nobody could possibly overlook it, would be very much attracted to her. In a short few years she would be that much older. And ages became very confused these days . . .

The song came to a sudden end, lilting off into the air. Ruby opened her eyes. From where Val stood, they seemed to glow as she asked, "That was a nice one, wasn't it, Nick?"

He wrote on a moment longer. Then he looked up. Something clutched at Valerie with the look he bent on the girl.

"Lovely, just lovely," he said. And when all at once his hand brushed her cheek, then smoothed back her flaming hair, Val stopped breathing. Fury flared, and contempt. Such an obvious, worn-out ploy from his bag of tricks. She hated herself for having fallen for it in the night. She should have been above that. Now, in the glare of daylight, she knew precisely why that gesture had affected her so shatteringly. It was Barry's gesture for her alone; he did it often. It was being separated from Barry that had done it. And what happened last night was clearly a case of transference, having nothing to do with McKenzie, who ought to be ashamed for involving that young, inexperienced girl who scarcely knew what was happening to her.

Ruby's face was radiant, and Nick McKenzie ought to be shot!

Val stepped onto the scene with a faint cough that brought their heads around together, Ruby's smile disintegrating. "I'm sorry if I'm breaking in," she began, her voice scratchy, "but I was thinking—"

"Leave that to me," he said. "How's the ankle?"

She flushed, answering, "Very well, thank you."

"Thought so. Doc McKenzie's magic touch." He twinkled up at her, his lips quirking. She went taut with rage, bursting with the need to hold her tongue. "Anything else ailing you?" he persisted, still grinning.

"My fanbelt!" she exploded, pouring her fury into the word. "You *said* you'd hunt one up, and now—"

"And now I'm playing games, ri-ight?"

He was teasing mercilessly, and she felt on the edge of tears. But then he rose to his feet, reaching a hand down to Ruby. She grasped it readily and he pulled her up to his side with a lazy smile.

"Great work hour, wasn't it?" he addressed Ruby, as if he'd forgotten Valerie entirely.

"I remember another, Nick," the girl said, eagerness trembling in her voice. "Would you like to hear it?"

Val thought she might as well touch her forehead to the

ground and inquire, "Would Lord and Master care for the belly dance now?"

Lord and Master seemed to be thinking it over, but decided, "Later, Ruby. I'd better drive down to your dad's place and see about this belt for her car. Want to come along?"

"Oh, yes—but can't we ride Sunny together?"

"The horse? What's wrong with the car?"

The girl merely shrugged. Val could have told him what was wrong. Bucket seats are nowhere near as intimate as a man and girl on the same horse.

Nick said, "Well, I guess so—why not?"

Valerie fell back as they moved together to where Sunny was indulging in a last nibble of grass. The horse was untethered, and in seconds Ruby was upon him, using Nick's cupped hands for a stirrup. When Nick leaped up behind her, Val saw her lounge against him as she handed him the reins. He wheeled the horse around at once, and only then remembered Val.

"Oh, say, there's a coffee pot, probably still warm, over in the cabin. Made it while you were asleep."

Her eyes flickered. She'd heard nothing.

He grinned again. "Did you know you sleep with your mouth open?"

Ruby laughed, as Nick nudged Sunny into a canter, winking at Val over his shoulder.

For a long, raging moment Val stared after them, her violet eyes intent. Then she went to find Patty and the children, determined to throw off the blanket of mindless confusion that he'd left her with yet another time.

The children, deeply involved piling stones into heaps, greeted her with shining faces, excitement in their voices explaining their building enterprises. "We're making this bi-ig fort, Val," Peter announced, "and it's where the pioneers are going to fend off the Indians—"

"And tomorrow," Gillian added breathlessly, "we're going to build an Indian village with teepees and—"

"Oh, but, children, we won't be here tomorrow. We'll be starting back home—"

"When?" Peter stood erect, his face fallen.

"Later today, I hope, dear—"

"Oh, noo-ooo—" he cried, Gillian lending her voice at once. "We don't want to go, we're having so much fun—"

"But, sweetheart, your daddy is expecting you." She knew even as she spoke that she had darkened their day. She saw Peter's lower lip jut slowly forward as his eyes slid from her face. He would not look at her, even when she cajoled him with promises of fun on the homebound journey. When he spoke, his voice came choked with tears.

"I'm not going. I like it here. I like *him*. Mr. McKenzie."

"Me, too," Gillian piped. "Oh, Valerie, do we have to go to Daddy?"

Val's heart sank. She felt like the evil witch in a fairy tale trying to make them understand that Barry loved them, and really wanted them with him.

Suddenly Gillian sobbed, "I want my mommy—"

Peter turned his back abruptly, and Val, watching the heave of his small shoulders, knew the boy was crying, too. It was a terrible moment. She had never realized how deep was the children's aversion to their father, and she was at a loss how to turn things around. For the immediate present, however, she lightened her tone and drew them slowly back to their fort construction, playing along with them for a time, until their enthusiasm rebounded. Not until she heard their first laughter did she leave them alone, moving disconsolately toward Patty's cabin—where she found *her* in tears.

"*Now* what?" she muttered, near the end of her rope.

"How can you ask? Didn't you see them?"

"Listen here," Val snapped, "if I hear one more reference to 'them' or 'him' or 'her' I just might hand you your head!"

"You're doing it already! And what are *you* so mad about?"

"*I'm not mad!*" she shouted. "I'm just annoyed. And so sick of this place I can't get away soon enough!"

"This morning you said it was beautiful!"

"*It* is! It's the company that goes out of its way to be nasty! The man's a boor. I don't see how you can even imagine yourself in love with him. He's a big-mouthed nothing! He has no charm, no class, no culture—" She stopped, her brows snapping together. "What the devil is he, anyway? What does he do with all that music? What's he writing down? What's the singing about? And that stupid fipple flute?"

Patty groaned and dried her tears. "You're wrong about everything. He's brilliant, this 'boor' you're knocking. He's a musicologist. He has a doctorate in it. He teaches—"

"Oh? You never said."

"What's to say when you're in love? What difference can it make? He's been traveling all over the States to remote places, gathering songs that have come down for generations but have never been committed to paper. And *she* has to be the one around here who knows them all. Sometimes I think she makes them up!"

"She? Ruby?"

"Her. Her people started out in West Virginia, and Kentucky, and Tennessee, way back. Her great-great grandmothers; she must've had dozens of them! And all those songs, apparently, have come down right through the years. Believe it, she can go on singing to him for the next century!"

She sniffed back a few more tears. "Nick's a photographer, too. He's taken a lot of shots around here—you know, sunrise, sunset things—to use in a book with the music. *And her on that horse*, too! See what I mean?"

Valerie grew thoughtful for a moment. "No, I don't. Anyway, get dressed, we'll have some breakfast."

"Who can eat?"

"Patty!" Valerie nearly screamed it, and for a tense moment the girl stared back at her in silence. Slowly she reached for a pair of jeans, drooping onto the floor. She worked them up her slender hips absently. Then she felt about under her bunk, found a couple of jerseys, dropped one, elbowed into the other, her eyes remaining distant throughout. All the while, Valerie had not moved. When Patty looked up, Val's face was almost severe.

"Are you finally ready?" she asked.

Patty hesitated. "Why won't you tell me—*what are you so mad about?*"

"Would you mind letting me alone?" she cried. She spun around and headed for the promised coffee pot.

When Patty caught up with her minutes later, Valerie had it heated and ready. Wordlessly she poured a mugful and handed it over. Patty received it in silence. Then with a sidelong glance, and from a safe distance, she spoke guardedly. "I never saw you like this before. I guess Barry would be surprised."

Chapter Nine

COFFEE AND SOME buns that Valerie found among Nick's provisions were all she had stomach for after that. Patty rummaged and found a jar of jam to go with hers. They did not talk, but Val was so uncomfortably aware of her cousin's furtive glances that, breakfast over, she sent her off to pack, under threats of annihilation.

She knew the girl would not, that she would lie down on her bunk and sulk. For the moment she did not care, for in the end she would have to pack for her anyway. Meanwhile, there had come this pressing need to be out of range of Patty's eyes. The girl had gotten under her skin with those snide cracks of hers. *Naturally* she was mad. And irritated. And impatient to get back to Barry again! Patty should know that without trying to make something out of nothing.

For a time, she watched the children at their fort-building, seemingly the only people in this place who weren't sniping at each other, in spite of what must lie heavy on their little hearts—that threat hanging over them, and threat it apparently was, of being returned to Barry. Try as she might, she could not dispel the feeling that the situation hung like a storm cloud over the future.

Wandering off thoughtfully, she poked around the old miners' cabins without venturing inside. They were, as Nick had warned, a mass of webs and dust and fallen beams, no doubt filled with everything that crawled. They smelled musty and dank and uninviting, and it occurred to her that Nick's own cabin and the one Patty was using must have been that way, too, before he came. He had put a lot of effort into making it livable. But Patty's? Since obviously Patty hadn't cleaned up her own, Nick must have done it for her, possibly in desperation as the only way to keep her from moving in with him. But why this farthest one from his? Why not the one next door, for instance, she wondered, wandering off in the other direction, toward the trail by which he must return. Did it have anything to do with that somewhat suggestive remark he'd made to Ruby the previous night when she'd protested about riding home in the dark? "It wasn't too dark all those other times...." So the girl stayed—at times—and very late...

A fair enough reason why he'd gone to all the trouble of fixing up a place for Patty, if only to provide himself and Ruby with peace and quiet and privacy for work? Or whatever...

Oh, who cares! She turned her thoughts off irritably. And what's keeping him? Surely it shouldn't take until nearly noon to pick up a fanbelt and get back!

Actually, it took even longer. It was well after one before they returned, and by the time Valerie heard Sunny's leisurely clip-clopping up the trail, she was frantic. She had managed a meal for the children and Patty, using some Spam and eggs from Nick's supply, but she had picked at hers because Patty was still shooting those oblique looks her way. Now as Nick rode into the clearing with Ruby still leaning against him as if she hadn't shifted once since they'd left, Valerie made a mental note to be sure to grab a bite before they left, because once they were on the road she meant to keep driving as long as conditions permitted.

She moved across the clearing and was half-running, half-limping toward them before Nick dismounted. He turned to offer a hand to Ruby who was singing in the same thin voice, and did not stop even as she dropped to the ground. Valerie felt again like an intruder, but this time she did not care.

"Nick! You have it?" Not for a moment had she entertained the idea that he might *not* have it. But when his expression went blank, her heart dropped like a stone. "The fanbelt, Nick—"

"Oh, yes, of course."

"Oh, good!"

"I mean—the fanbelt, of course—but sorry, for a Jaguar it's not to be had. It'll be coming up from Cedar City in a few days. We were lucky to find a service center Jake knew about down there that had it. We phoned and they're putting one aside for us. A young friend of mine is coming through that way. He'll bring it."

She thought he was fooling, teasing, *tormenting* her in that way he had. She tried desperately to believe that!

"But I can't stay, I've got to leave!" she breathed finally.

"Tough luck! What's wrong? The accommodations not good enough?"

He turned abruptly to the girl. "Okay, now, Ruby, you've got something to do?"

"Your cabin, I guess."

"I took care of that," Val said casually, and bridled the next moment, seeing Ruby's face go taut.

"That's my work," the girl said.

The mood she was in, Val could not resist. "Not when I sleep in the master's bed!"

"Oh, for crying out loud!" Nick exploded. "Okay, Ruby, maybe you'd better trot on home after all. Your mom'll need some help."

It was a dismissal, but Ruby reminded him, "You wanted to work some more, Nick. You said so."

"Another day. Something tells me the atmosphere around here is going to be less than conducive for a while. Run along now, honey. Come on, I'll help you up."

"Don't need it!" she muttered and with the aid of an

ancient tree stump, she sprang aboard Sunny's broad back
for the gallop home. Her last black glare was for Val, who
smothered a sudden urge to shout after her, "Thank your
father for this!" But she saved her ire for Nick instead.

"Now *she's* mad!" he muttered.

"No more than I."

"You're always mad. You make a career of mad. It's as
if you took a course and went into the business!"

This was getting nowhere. "What's the story on my fanbelt?"

"Just what I said. Jake had nothing and we rode over to
a couple of places—"

"Where were they—London?"

"Sarcasm, after a morning like this, happens not to be
my dish of tea, Val. You know the distances between places
here. And the midday heat. We were even more anxious
to find you that damned belt than you are so you can be
off! This place sounds like a running cat fight, you and
Patty—"

"And Ruby, don't let's forget Ruby!"

"At least she doesn't yell! And give her credit, she remembered about Doug down at Canyon de Chelly—"

"Who's Doug? Where's Canyon de—*wha-at?*"

"Doug Ledyard. One of my students last year back East.
An anthropology major. We drove out together, in two cars,
that is. I was looking for likely material, and stumbled on
it here when I ran into Ruby. And Doug went on to Canyon
de Chelly, capital C-h-e-l-l-y. That's Navajo country. In
Arizona—"

"Arizona! Nick! If you can't find a fanbelt here, what
makes you think the Navajos make them? And who needs
it down there?"

He shook his head in disbelief. "Do you ever—*have* you
ever allowed anyone to finish what they start before you
begin nit-picking it apart?"

"All right! Finish. Just leave out the guided tours and
biographical sketches of your friends, *and* the spelling class,
Professor! What's this got to do with my fanbelt?"

"Oh, nothing." He shrugged. "Except that Doug wrote me a few days ago he'll be coming by this way in a week to ten days and I shot him off a letter right away to be sure to pick up the fanbelt when he goes through Cedar City. He'll be continuing on to Nevada—"

"Ten days! Did you say *ten* days?" Val's hands cupped her cheeks. She stared blankly before her. "Ten days around here?"

There was a small pause, which grew to a large pause, very large and very strained until gradually Nick swam up again into Val's line of vision...swam because her eyes were brimming. His clipped tone broke the back of the silence.

"Sorry, it's the best I could do. Sweated all over the landscape doing it, I don't mind pointing out!"

He turned and started away from her with long angry strides. She hesitated, then sprinted after him. "Nick, please—I *am* sorry. I've been pretty ungrateful—"

"I couldn't agree with you more!" he said, still walking.

"All right, don't get carried away," she answered, stiffening again. "It just hit me hard, that's all. There's so much I have to get back to. My business and—Barry, of course."

"Of course."

They were nearing his cabin when the impulse seized her. It was now or never. "Nick, wait—before you go. You're as anxious to see the last of us as I am to leave."

"Right on target."

"If you could speed up that fanbelt delivery, you would, wouldn't you?"

"I'd turn somersaults!"

"That's nice. Now then, how far is Cedar City?"

He stared down, his eyes narrowing.

"*No way*, Val Sheppard! Somersaults, yes. But no way will I drive a couple hundred miles there and back after everything else I've done and all the work time I've lost. My time here is limited enough as it is. I have some speaking engagements coming up next month, and another stopoff before that in Montana. You can just manage as best you

can, and if I can put up with you, you can put up with me.
But bear in mind, if I don't get some peace and quiet around
here, I am going to up-end a couple of squabbling females
and warm their hides!"

Val's lids stung again, this time in anger. But she suppressed that quite well, biting her lip until she almost drew
blood. She needed one more favor.

"Very well, then. But I have to call New York."

"Oh, yes. The bridegroom waiteth, out of his mind by
now over you and the children. Well, you know where the
phone is."

"You know I won't go there alone."

"Oh, the old paranoia again. I'll have to drive you there
anyway—with the house full of guests, we'll need some
more supplies. Would the kids like to come?"

Without awaiting her answer, he shouted across the open
space, "Hey, kids, want to come and talk to your dad on
the phone?"

Val, conscious of her own sudden tension, saw their
small faces turn from play, two pairs of wide eyes staring
back, unsmiling. It seemed minutes before Peter wailed,
"Aw, do we have to?"

Val's stomach knotted, *wishing* Nick hadn't started that.

"Heck, no, you don't have to," he yelled back. "But you
won't be seeing him for some time now, Pete, old man, and
I thought—" He broke off seeing their faces blossom with
smiles.

"We're staying here?" Peter asked.

"A while. Like ten days, maybe—" Nick responded.

"Oh, boy!" Now they hugged each other jumping up and
down.

"So? Don't you think you ought to talk to your father,
kids?"

"Naw, we don't want to go—"

"Got a message for him? Something for Val to tell him?"
They shook their heads wildly, grinning from ear to ear.

"What if he asks for you?"

"He won't," Peter answered promptly, and Gillian sang

out over and over, "We don't care, we don't care, we don't care..." Until Val put a stop to it, calling out, "All right, you don't have to come." Their "Goody, goody, goody" was ringing in her ears when she turned to Nick. "Was that inquisition necessary? Wasn't it enough that you invited them and they declined? What were you probing for?"

She would never forget the grimness of the look he gave her. "Yeah," he said, "call it probing. I was just wondering what in hell kind of a guy you're so hung up on whose own kids can't stand him."

Then as she fell back, too stunned for speech, he muttered, "Have to tell Patty to keep an eye on them. We don't want them around that digging. Where is she? Oh, yes, she's there, all right!"

His glance had swept the clearing to where nature had provided Patty with her own private pedestal, a giant rock on which she languished now, Val noted, wearing perhaps the largest sunglasses, and skimpiest bikini, in fashion history. Val thought that with everything else, this entire hideous excursion was getting weirder by the minute. Still, there was a need not to antagonize Nick any more than necessary; she was wholly dependent on his good will and, never mind what he thought of Barry, she needed his favors.

"I'll need my clothes and the children's," she remarked.

"We'll pick up your bags on the return ride."

"When do we go?"

"When you're ready."

"Well"—she owed him—"don't you want a cup of coffee first? I made a fresh pot."

Nick's glance swung to her, his brows skirting his hairline. "Thought you'd never ask. Does that mean you care?"

"That means there's fresh coffee. Do you want it or don't you?"

"Well! That's more like the Valerie Sheppard of the honeyed tones I know! Tough, feisty, with the disposition of a gila monster! And, hey, I forgot to ask how you slept last night."

Her eyes, avoiding his, slitted. But she decided to ignore that one. Inside the cabin, handing him his mug, it occurred to her he looked tired and dusty from the long ride, and a sliver of guilt actually wedged in there somewhere behind her pressing urge to be gone.

She was not looking forward to encountering the Jordans again, with or without Nick present. It was like an incursion into no-man's-land. But she would take that risk and more, if only to hear Barry's calming tones. Barry was contact with the real world again. Barry was like—touching bases once more after Nick's wholly unjustified remarks, and that awful shocked look on his face *daring* to question the "kind of a guy...whose own kids can't stand him."

What would a character like Nick, loose and unattached, know about the agonies Claire had put Barry through? And how all the children ever knew was whatever Claire must have told them, poisoning their minds against their father. Still, there was a job to be done when they were all together again. She *must* get through to Barry that he was only reinforcing Claire's lies, unless he began to exhibit more love and spend more time with Peter and Gillian. Oh, but that was for the future...and this was now, today, and she must put all that out of her mind and get on with her phoning. She would phone Aunt Emily, too; even *her* voice would be reassuring. And of course, she would call Deedee at The Rain Forest just to see if everything was under control, though there wasn't much she could do about it if it wasn't.

She would leave Barry's call for the last, and best, and what with the two-hour zone difference, by the time she got through to him, he could be quitting for the day.

Then Nick decided arbitrarily on a second cup of coffee. "You make a good cup, Val. You'll have to leave your recipe."

"Oh, come on," she grumbled, impatient with his games.

"Hey, wasn't there a package of buns around here some-place?"

"There are two left."

"I'll take them."

She brought them from the cabin to where he'd wandered out to sprawl on a rock in the shade. She made a great show of glancing at her watch. Then she stood back, arms folded, watching him take his time. On the second bun, she began pacing up and down. After another heavy glance at her watch, he finally growled, "I get indigestion when I gulp these things."

"Jake sells Alka-Seltzer?"

"Any more coffee in that pot?"

"No. You've had enough. Especially if you're the indigestion type."

He popped the last of the bun into his mouth, chewed with exasperating deliberation, swallowed, and reminded her, "Never had a day's stomach trouble until this nightmare began. First, Patty, then you—"

"Doesn't Ruby fit in there someplace?"

Their eyes clashed on that and his went inscrutable. She wished, suddenly, she had left that out. "You had your chance to speed things up, but no, you wouldn't take the extra day to drive to Cedar City—"

"And miss all this entertainment? I'd be crazy."

He grinned, licking the sugar from his fingers and wiping them on his dungarees. "They serve napkins where I come from."

"They *have* napkins where I come from. Where did you hide yours?"

He chuckled, rising at last. Without a word, he stalked over to where Patty had shifted to a more fetching posture. The children clamored to Nick at once. "Nick, Nick, look what we got! We built an Indian tepee."

"Hey, that's great! Now you be good kids and listen to Aunt Patty—"

"*Aunt* Patty?" The girl bolted upright, outraged.

"Get back. You're positively ravishing sprawled out there with your mouth shut! Just keep an eye on the kids and see that they don't go—"

"Aw, we know," Peter said. "We don't go near the mine shaft!"

"Right, and maybe I can find you some Indian feathers at the store!"

"Where are you going?" Patty sulked predictably. "Can't I go?"

"You've got somebody to call in New York? Your mother, maybe?"

Patty didn't answer. Her chin puckered, and Val knew there were tears behind those owlish lenses.

"You've got a reprieve," she comforted her. "We're staying a while. Ten days perhaps."

"Big deal."

Then they were on their way, the Land Rover bouncing along the stony trail, but far, far from the pace Val had expected.

"Is this the best we can do?" she asked once when he seemed almost to crawl. Frustration was churning up a storm in her. On her lap her hands clenched and unclenched.

When she began drumming her knees, he said, "You're in a hurry? The phone works twenty-four hours a day."

"Does it? With everything else that's been going wrong, it just might break down before we get there. Can't you speed it up a little?"

He rammed the pedal so hard she fell back with a snap. "Some people manage to enjoy the beauty of this trail."

"It's all cliffs."

"And sunlight shafting through."

"It's dark and eerie down here."

"Look up! The sky's brilliant. And you might just glimpse a flying squirrel among the firs at the top. Or a formation of wild ducks. Or any number of creatures scurrying around. There's life all around you!"

She remained determinedly silent until he growled, "About all you'd see are the snakes!"

"All *right!*" she snapped. "I am totally chastened. Now can we get on a little faster?"

For half an hour after, he did not so much as glance her way. Val thought, good, he's gotten the message. She settled back in her seat, satisfied he was beginning to understand that they operated on totally different wavelenghts, and what happened the night before was no indication that she was a Ruby or a Patty. The image he was trying to project bored her to tears.

He stared straight ahead through the windshield, his jaw

stern, hard. Even the beard could not hide that, nor soften the effect of the slight hawklike curve of his nose. Not a bad nose, she conceded. Very much in line with the rest of him. His hands on the wheel, for instance, brown and tough. Strong, but curiously, an artist's hands. Large. With a wide spread. At her back, they had felt . . .

"What are you looking at?"

His rumbling taunt stunned her. She hadn't realized she had been studying him. Or that he was aware. She reddened, stammering, "The—scenery?"

He laughed, shredding her thin defense. "Yeah. Like the scenery last night. Not too bad, huh?"

"That's ridiculous. What could I do about it—"

"Slap me, claw my cheeks, scream. But I know, I know, I was stronger than you and all that."

"And a damned sight more arrogant," she reminded him.

"That, too," he conceded easily. "But—it was nice, anyway, Val. Agreed?"

"You've got *more* gall!"

"My share," he acknowledged. "Now, bottle up that rage," he added as they rounded the final bend before Jake's store, "and be real nice. This is the man who's ordered your fanbelt for you."

"This is the man who messed up all my plans. Your wonderful friend."

"Believe it," he muttered.

"You'll see. Watch the way they treat me."

Minutes later, Nick's mouth twisted in a downward grin. Jake and Millie rose jointly from their porch chairs to greet them.

"Hey, there, pardner, nice to see you back!" Jake called, slouching down the steps. The woman, smoothing her shapeless dress, smiled, displaying several toothless gaps back of her pale lips. Together their glances shifted to Valerie, but the expected hardening of their faces never happened.

"Sorry to hear 'bout your trouble, miss," Jake said.

"Oh, are you?" she answered, thrown off balance, but

cool. "*You* wouldn't have any idea what may have caused that fanbelt to come off?"

"Oh—well, 'most anything. Happens sometime."

"Strange, it's never happened to any other car I've driven."

"Always a first time, I reckon."

She would have abandoned the fruitless parrying there, but Nick's eyes rankled. She had to go on, though lightly now.

"You certainly knew what you were talking about, Jake, telling me I'd never make it to Jordan's Hole, didn't you? Why, if it hadn't been for Nick just happening along at the right time, I'd have been stranded out on that trail just the way you said."

His eyes, she thought, bit hard into hers but his smile never faltered. "Told you right, miss, didn't I? Even if you hadn't broke down, you'd 'a gone straight by that canyon opening and never knew it was there. It's why I warned you out'n that canyon, didn't I? Told you you got no business in it with the young ones at night."

Val's head reeled. The man had an answer for everything. Nick was openly amused now, and to help matters along, Millie edged closer and spoke up in saccharine tones.

"Now, Jake, don't you go keepin' the folks out in this here heat. Mus' be near a hundred. Y'all come inside. Ruby'll git you a cola. Or anything you want."

"Thank you, Millie," Nick said, "that's nice of you. Actually Miss Sheppard has to make some phone calls."

"Well, then, you just go talk to Ruby while she's doin' that. She likes comp'ny. She's in there ironin' those shirts o' your'n—"

"Oh, say, they don't need ironing." He sounded embarrassed.

"Well, she likes things nice for you."

As Val walked up the steps thoroughly confused, she thought no one would guess they had just seen Nick that morning, or that Ruby had nestled for hours in his arms on Sunny's back. She could not wait to get into the phone booth to be alone with Barry for a while. Once again, Barry meant hard, solid reality. This other thing here, this weird distortion of the simple facts, was beginning to get to her.

It took some seconds for her eyes to adjust from sunlight to shadow. As details emerged from the haze, she saw that, for all its dilapidated exterior, the store within seemed fairly well stocked. In a moment Ruby emerged, too, standing before an ironing board at the rear of the store. Warm currents of air from an electric fan set the tendrils of her hair trembling against her creamy skin, and once again Valerie was struck by the girl's beauty. Even the blankness of her expression at sight of Val could not affect that.

They were hardly inside when her mother shrilled, "Let that be now, Ruby. Go get Mr. McKenzie somethin' real cold to drink. And I reckon the lady'll want a glass too. The phone is back there, miss."

Valerie glanced around for a booth and found to her dismay an open wall phone. She looked around, but nobody made any move to grant her privacy. Millie was drawing chairs out from an old-fashioned ice-cream parlor table, the only one there for passing tourists.

"Now you jus' make yourself to home, Mr. McKenzie." Then she went to help Ruby with glasses and soda.

A little later, when Valerie had sorted out her coins and begun dialing, she glanced back over her shoulder to see Ruby in the chair her mother had placed next to Nick's. The woman hovered a little longer, then went to join Jake at a fly-specked counter near the door.

Val's first call went through to Deirdre and the talk was terse. A few minor business matters were discussed; a wrong shipment of orchids which had arrived, a Brazilian nerve plant which had not, the latest hassle with Simba the cat, through whose perseverance the world was minus one angel fish. "I pasted him one, of course!" Deedee assured her. "But other than that, you've hardly been missed, honey!"

"Thanks a heap!" Val laughed, then rattled off some explicit directions about the orchids, the nerve plant, and

Simba who was to be banished upstairs eternally if he so much as . . .

She hung up aware of the listening silence. As if every word she had spoken had been of paramount interest to those present. Only Nick sipped his cola as if he hadn't heard a word or cared.

She turned her back and called Aunt Emily, conscious that her audience was in for a treat, considering Aunt Em's habit of screeching into the phone whenever she spoke long distance.

"Darling!" Aunt Em cried, her voice carrying straight into the room. "Finally! Oh, Val. You've found her! Is she all right?"

"She's fine, Em. No . . . nothing bad . . ."

"You're hiding something. I can tell from the way you're talking."

Val groaned, then struggled to reassure Emily. "Patty's fine. Believe me. Who? Oh, Mr. McKenzie. Yes, he has been very nice to her, considering."

"Considering . . . wh-what?"

"Considering he's just delighted that I came to take her off his hands."

There was a pregnant silence. "What's that supposed to mean, Valerie?"

Val suppressed an urge to laugh. Emily sounded indignant, as if she were speculating whether Nick had used, and was now discarding Patty. She put a quick end to Emily's fears with a rapid rundown of the car trouble and the necessary delay. "And you're not to worry. I'm with her. Nothing's going to happen."

"Oh, you don't know that girl!" Emily warned. "And the things she does to men!"

"The things she does to boys, Aunt Em!" Val said sharply. "This one is *a man!*"

That escaped Val so clumsily, she wanted to bite her tongue. Her cheeks flamed when she hung up and began at once to dial Barry. She had not dared to face that waiting silence. She knew without looking that Nick would be grinning back of his beard, Jake and Millie would be exchanging enigmatic looks, and Ruby . . . oh, what did it matter?

Barry picked up his phone after several rings and she forgot Ruby! In her instant breathlessness she heard a chair scrape, and with a quick sidelong glance saw Nick leaving through the screen door. Ruby was at his heels. Decent of him, she thought. Too bad the other two didn't follow. Then, at Barry's shout of pleasure, they hardly mattered.

"Finally!" Barry said. "I've been thinking of you all day—"

"And night?" she teased.

"Ah . . . yes, nights, too. What's going on there? Where are you? Heading home?"

"How I wish!" Swiftly she acquainted him with the situation and the expected delay. "But the children are fine. In fact, they're enjoying every minute of their stay."

"Ha! So am I!" He chuckled.

Val backed away from that remark. It was a joke, of course; Barry's kind of a joke. But she was getting a little weary of it. It hadn't really been funny the first time. She thrust it out of mind, and asked, "Are you busy, darling? Have you been getting things done?"

"Working like—oh, damn—"

There'd come a clicking on the line, and a voice breaking in. Val wailed, "Oh, no, I hope we're not being cut off."

"'Course not—" It was a woman's lazy drawl and Barry broke in crisply, "Please get off the line."

"*You* get off an' come on back, lover . . . lonesome—"

"Hang up, will you? Oh, Christ!" The last muffled and angry. And with that, it blasted over Valerie that the voice was on *Barry's own line*. The extension, in fact, beside his bed.

"That's—Ivy, isn't it, Barry?" Her lips barely shaped the words, so stiff they had become.

"I'm not denying it," he groaned. "Ivy, will you kindly— oh, hang on a minute, Val." She heard his phone clatter to the desk and his steps receding. She picked up their muffled movement again on the bedroom carpeting. Then his voice, cajoling, "Better hand me that phone, Ivy girl. You're really not your best now—"

There was a sound of tussling, and her voice dimming out. "Wanna see my best . . . lover—" Then he was back on the line again.

"Okay now, darling, I took it from her."

"She's—in your bedroom, isn't she?"

"How do I keep her out?"

"You phone Jon, that's how."

"In Texas? They had a battle after that other day, remember? He flew back. I think they're splitting. That's what she came by to tell me. Feeling pretty low about it, too."

"She doesn't sound it."

"She had a drink or two." In the background Ivy sounded incoherent.

"Barry," Val said, "you know what she's like. Why did you give it to her?"

"Honey—" He sounded *not* annoyed, but impatient. "Can't we continue this another time? I've got my hands full here."

He did sound harried, but Val stiffened. "Anything you say, Barry. I'm sorry I called."

"Now, don't. Not you, too! Listen, I was delighted you called. I hoped you would quickly. I wanted to tell you, there's something coming up in Phoenix next week that I want to attend. I'm thinking if I pick you and the kids up after the business is over, we can all come back together. We'll make it a holiday. We'll have a few days at Las Vegas or whatever. How does that grab you?"

"Mm, nice."

"Nice? How about, 'Ter-*rif*ic, Barry darling'?"

She laughed. "All right, terrific."

"That's more like it. Well, look, honey, what you've got to do is air-mail me a route up from Phoenix where the turnpikes end and the wilds begin, so I can rent a car and find you."

"I'll do that right away, Barry."

"And one more thing. I love you. And don't you ever forget it!"

She could not resist, "Did Ivy hear you say that?"

He chuckled. "Ivy, thank the Lord, is out like a light. When she wakes up, she won't remember a thing about it. Not even how she got into my bed, with all her clothes on including her shoes! And would you believe her sunglasses?"

Val laughed softly and Barry joined in. For a few seconds longer, they laughed together, but after they'd hung up, Val stood a very long time picturing Ivy Ashley, in Barry's bed, fully dressed, even to shoes and sunglasses. She tried very hard to see how funny it was.

As she headed resolutely for the porch, she was dimly aware of Jake and Millie watching her leave. She did not nod, though not from coldness. She was still back in New York, in Barry's bedroom. She pushed through the screen door and saw Nick leaning on a pillar.

She did not see Ruby. Not because the girl wasn't prominent enough, resting against the porch rail. But because for one blinding instant, her eyes and Nick's collided . . . and everything else faded from her mind.

Chapter Ten

SHE KNEW INTUITIVELY he had left earlier to afford her some privacy with Barry. Just as she knew now he had been waiting to read what he could from her face. For what reason, intuition failed her. But having read it, as his penetrating look attested, she knew it was futile to carry on any sort of pretense.

Her reaction was mixed; it was no affair of his, and yet if she could have talked, for the sake of sorting out her feelings, though it startled her she realized he was the only person around to whom she could have spelled it out.

Still, when he rumbled, "Everything okay?" she could only answer, "Oh, fine!" But she could not dredge up a smile to go with it. "In fact, he's to be in Phoenix next week on business. He'll come up this way and we'll all go home together—as soon as the Jaguar's ready."

Nick bit down hard on his pipe stem. She noticed that the pipe had not been lit.

Millie, who with Jake had joined the others on the porch, spoke up unexpectedly. "That your young man?"

"Uh, yes. Of course."

"Them his kids?"

Val bit her lip while Nick coughed and shifted position.

Valerie nodded an answer, anxious now to be gone. But Millie wanted more.

"You fixin' to marry him?"

"She just told you, Ma!" Ruby broke in, her voice strained. Val shot her a grateful look, though the girl did not meet it.

"Ain't told me nothin'," Millie said. "Anyway, I just ast a simple woman-to-woman question, is all."

It was Nick who broke it up. "If you're ready to go back, Val, why don't you wait in the car? I'll pick up a few groceries, and Indian feathers—"

"Oh, let me help you," she breathed, aghast at the prospect of finding herself alone with a Jordan. Any Jordan. When she followed him inside, Jake and Millie came, too. Only Ruby hung back, and seeing the wretchedness of her expression, Val felt a brief wave of sadness for her. Her mother had been an embarrassment.

Inside, she focused attention on the canned and packaged items. When she selected a box of powdered milk for the children, Nick remembered to order water. "We'll need several more drums early next week, Jake. With company coming—"

"Oh, yes," Val abruptly recalled, and asked Nick quietly about jotting down a route for Barry from Phoenix. "They pick up mail here, don't they?"

"Right," he said and lifted a road map from a rack near the door. Then he bought a pad, air-mail envelope, and stamp from Millie's "post office" counter and steered Valerie to the table where earlier he'd sat beside Ruby. She could feel the Jordan stares accompanying her all the way. Those slippery glances, subtle as airport floodlights, annoyed her so fiercely that she deliberately rattled her chair as close to Nick's as possible, pulling back sharply when their knees touched. Nick, faking shock, gasped. "Madam, is no man safe?"

Val flushed so warmly, she could barely blurt, "Would you get on with it, please?"

He grinned and bent over the paper, sketching a rough

map. "I'll jot down these route numbers and he can check them against the road map. Then when he gets past civilization . . . let's see, we'll pick him up here . . ." He paused, pen poised somewhere north of Cedar City. She waited, then glanced up to find a glint of mirth in his eyes. "Now, where do we put him down? Uh—how's the middle of Great Salk Lake?"

"You are not one bit funny!" She bit the words off impatiently.

"I thought I was hilarious. I mean, the possibilities—"

"Nick, please get finished," she whispered. "I cannot stand those stares I'm getting from Jake."

"That's a cast in his eye," he muttered back. "Anyway, they were both nice to you, weren't they? All right, then, we'll bring him right along to this store, Val. Because only the Jordans and their nearest neighbors know about this hole anyway. Jake will guide him in the rest of the way."

He finished swiftly after that, and turning the paper over, handed it to Valerie with his pen. "Add your own passionate phrases, that's not my department. I'll look away."

He did, but she did not. She did add a word about picking up an extra fanbelt for the car in case something went wrong. And then she scrawled, "See you soon, Love, Val." After that, she addressed the envelope and handed it to Nick who stamped it and gave it to Millie for mailing.

Val could not get outside fast enough, though the shadows there had begun to encroach. The ride to the clearing, she knew, would be gray and chill between the rearing black walls but a pleasant prospect by comparison.

Nick, carrying the groceries, opened the screen door for her, and she hurried through. She had gone down the steps and was nearly to the car before she saw Ruby loitering on the opposite side, the side that Val had to enter.

"Nick," she began, coming around to him at once. Val could not miss the tremor in her voice.

"Ruby!" Yes?"

"When do you want me again?"

He hesitated. "Well—" He opened the door and shoved

the groceries behind the front seat before continuing. "Let's see—"

"Tomorrow, Nick?"

"You know, Ruby, I've been looking over my material, and I've been thinking I've got about all I'm going to need."

"Oh, but I keep remembering more!"

"Mm, yes, of course." Val sensed he was hedging. "I just feel you've given me such a wealth of material, all those eastern hill-country tunes, and the western mining songs, sometimes versions nobody ever heard before, I'm sure. And they're all terrific. But I can't devote my whole book to one area. I'll be moving on north shortly."

"Will you, Nick?"

"Now, Ruby, you knew that."

"But there's still time. I mean, it's not over yet, Nick."

Val could feel him changing tack. "It's got to be over sometime, Ruby. And yes, I'll write you a check as I promised, for all your help. And your name is going to be right up there among the credits in my book. You've earned that—"

"Oh, I don't care about all that, Nick." An edge of panic sharpened her voice.

"All right," he said abruptly, "Come on over tomorrow. If there's no time for work—"

She seized on that. "Yes, I'll come. I'll bring the fresh laundry—"

She left them abruptly, storming up the steps. The screen door slammed so hard behind her, the dusk crackled with echoes. Val felt vastly relieved when Nick said, "All right, let's go."

As they headed up the trail, she could not throw off the pall that had settled over her. The emotional wrenches had come too swiftly on the heels of one another. Barry . . . Ivy . . . Ruby—it was too much.

In the end it was the girl she spoke of, because if she tried to cope with the other situation first, she might just come apart. It needed cooling first.

"She's in love with you," she said when they'd driven a time wordlessly.

"Hogwash!" But he'd picked up the reference instantly.

"Why do you say that? Because you encouraged it?"

"Oh, sure! Like I encouraged Patty!"

His tone was brusque, clipped off short.

"All right, you're home free on Patty!"

"Thanks. Damn bright of you to notice."

"That still leaves Ruby. Don't weasel out."

His answer was a muffled expletive that it was probably better she did not hear.

"Listen, Ruby's a nice kid. Someday she's going to be a beautiful woman. And she's not stupid. But unless she does something about her situation, by the time she's forty, she'll be her mother all over again. If she lived anyplace but here—"

"What's wrong with here? Some of the loveliest people come from Utah."

His lips clamped shut, obviously stifling a rush of annoyance. "Some of the loveliest people come from everywhere on the face of the earth!" he finally exploded. "Along with some other kinds. Jake and Millie seem decent enough. Only they inherited along with their land—which is no good for farming or mining or anything else much except for its scenic beauty—the irrational bitterness of the have-nots for the haves! Even those haves who managed to put one stone on top of another until they built themselves a good life.

"Jake must know there are plenty of tourists driving by his place. More would, and some might be persuaded to stay awhile, if he ever shaped up, took a paintbrush in hand, made a few repairs, most of which he could do alone, and offered them something to stay for! Then maybe there'd be incentive for Ruby to *do* something with herself, and a little money to do it with! And what I've been trying to get across to her is that her parents are hopeless, and she's going to have to do it on her own!"

"I see. And of course, she's jumped to all the wrong

conclusions. Well, it happens sometimes, when a man tells himself he's playing the kindly-uncle type."

"Watch it!"

"Only to find himself galloping off on a great white steed with his arms around the girl—"

"*That does it!*" He braked so sharply, Val jerked forward. "What's *that* for?"

"If nothing else'll shut you up! As soon as we left there, you got your needles out and began—embroidering me! Would you mind telling me why? No, I'll tell you! You came away so uptight after that phone call to Mr. Big-and-Important, you've got to take it out on someone! And I'm the handiest someone around!"

"I—I don't know what you're talking about! And I doubt you do, either." Her voice had gone hollow.

"You doubt, do you? I've seen longer faces on elephants, but not much!"

"I had a lovely talk with Barry. He—had a client with him, so we couldn't talk long, that's all."

"A client, was she? No, don't explain. I don't want to hear your troubles, lady. And you just stay off mine. Now if you're ready, we'll go on."

She leaned back in the seat, closing her eyes, as if that would block out the humiliation that suddenly seared so fiercely. Her cheeks felt hot and a clamminess spread to the roots of her hair. He'd been right, though she'd die before she'd tell him. She'd been dodging and ducking the Barry-Ivy thing like Punch's Judy, grasping at any straw, not to have to *think* about it.

Even now there were angles she could not face up to squarely. Though Ivy was a "lush," her drinking certainly hadn't begun to ruin that svelte figure. Perhaps one day it would, but meanwhile even her face was striking, with those high-fashion cheekbones framed by her soft ash-blonde hair, and her sensual mouth above the slight cleft in her chin. Even drunk, there'd been something in those eyes, too, that led one way—to the bedroom. Fully dressed, with shoes on, was after all a temporary condition...

Here Valerie acknowledged a mounting surge of anger. How long had Ivy been gravitating to Barry like that? When had it begun? And why? Had he let it happen out of loneliness, because Claire was never home? Or . . . For the first time, Val wondered if it were the other way around. Who had pursued whom?

Absurd, really, she thought. Here was Barry about to come all the way up from Phoenix to be with her and the children for the return trip, even though the children made him nervous. Didn't that prove something?

Didn't it?

Well, *answer*, heart! Head! Say something!

Beside her, Nick was taking his temper out on the car, aiming at every hole or rut along the rough trail. The ride was jarring the daylights out of her. Her eyes remained shut, her head flung back. When the sob broke from her throat, she threw herself forward, flinging a hand to her lips.

"Oh, for heaven's sake!" he breathed. Impatient? Concerned? He slowed, then slowed some more and pulled over.

"Rapped your knuckles kind of hard, did I?"

She bent almost to her lap, shaking her head vigorously. Now both hands covered her face, but the tears trickled between.

"It has nothing to do with you," she gasped.

"Good. Then I can offer my shoulder with no strings attached."

"Don't need it," she mumbled, and on an impulse opened the door and stepped to the ground. "If you don't mind—"

"Help yourself." He turned his back, took out his pipe, and went through the lighting routine. She had needed to be alone, she thought, just long enough to pull herself together. But when she'd moved a short distance into the shadows, it was still not working.

She leaned against the cliff face, listening to the silence, and the evening chorus of birds. The aroma of Nick's tobacco drifted her way and with it, unexpectedly, something of his presence.

She wished she'd never met him. He was an intrusion. He did not approve of Barry, and his mocking eyes and quirking lips showed it. Not that he had any call to act *that* supercilious. Deny it, fight it all he wished, he'd let the Ruby thing get out of hand badly. And for a man of his age, and experience, that was a pretty dumb thing to do— *unless he wanted to!*

That irritated her now. It did not concern her, really, but it, too, kept intruding, and rather pointlessly, in their discussions. Or was "battles" a better word? *Why on earth did he provoke her so?* Perhaps because she could not open her mouth with the most superficial reference to Barry without drawing barbs from him. He was unnerving. And at a worrisome time like this, a mind muddler...

And suddenly he stood beside her. "It's getting chilly."

"I—didn't feel it," she whispered.

"The shoulder's still poised."

"It's wasting its time."

A small wind swooped from above, ruffling her hair. She grasped her bare arms and hugged herself against the cold she had just denied. His arm came around her, and she stiffened, for the flutter of a bat's wing. His hand was warm on her skin, gripping her shoulder. "Want to go back?"

"Not—yet. Patty'll be a bit much."

"It's what I thought. Like to sit in the car?"

She shook her head. "It's serene out here. In the dusk. Do you mind?"

"It's destroying me." He dropped his arm and sauntered back to the car, to return with a spare wool shirt to toss around her.

"Thanks," she said, and the next instant reeled at that same dizzying aroma that was so markedly him. Tobacco, sweat, soap—whatever, she thought, casting it from her mind even as she hugged the huge thing around her. He was scrounging about in the growth edging the trail. Bafflingly. Until she saw him gathering bits and pieces of dried and fallen branches. She watched wordless, but with a murmur of excitement, as he shaved some to kindling with his pocket knife. In a hollow where the rock walls fell back a way, he laid his foundation, piling wood upon kindling upon shavings. When he'd finally flicked his lighter to the whole, he glanced abruptly across its reddish glare, and her breath died. Whatever it was that he read in her watching eyes seemed suddenly to please him.

"Come closer," he said. "You'll soon be warm."

She moved in woodenly and knelt in the circle of heat. He came around and sat beside her cross-legged. For a measureless span, no word passed between them. Now and then when he tossed fresh wood on the flames, sending myriad sparks shafting to the fading ribbon of sky, the crackle that filled the silence seemed only to expand it. The hush was eerie, muffling the scurry of night creatures in the brush, and the still-persistent twittering of birds. Finally Valerie heard nothing except the fury and thunder at her temples . . . and wondered if he heard that, too . . .

But he was humming. She became aware only dimly as her pulse simmered down, and knew instinctively it would be one of Ruby's mountain songs because his head was so full of them now.

"One of hers?" she asked.

"Mm." He did not resume the melody.

"What's it called."

"It has no name yet. I call it 'Song-without-words-for-those-special-moments-in-life-when-nothing-makes-sense-and-you-wonder-what-brought-you-to-such-an-impasse'!"

"It's a little long," she whispered, "but as good as any . . . nothing does make sense—"

She broke off. His hand had covered hers where it rested on the ground between them. She did not resist.

"What's he like?" he asked with an abruptness that stunned the breath from her. It took several seconds to respond, and then her voice wavered. "What's—who like?"

"Come on, play it straight for once."

Still she hesitated, dodging a crazy compulsion to answer that which she did not know.

"Why do you ask?" she parried.

"Curious. The kids hate him. You love him. It doesn't add up."

"I loved him long before there were any kids," she said. "He was my first—"

"Lover," he supplied when she left it unsaid.

"All right. My first and only."

"It's getting clearer," he said. "Women, they tell me, have a fixation about the first one—all their lives, they tell me."

"Do they also tell you it can be very *real*? The love, I mean."

"But he ditched you!"

She drew her hand back sharply. "You don't know what *she* was like. The ends she went to. You're jumping to conclusions."

"The kids love her. They hate him."

"She's poisoned their little minds. I'm going to change all that."

"You believe that?"

She felt his hand closing on hers again, and once again let it remain even while answering impatiently, "I really don't want to talk about it."

"Good. Neither do I. Besides, you've answered my questions." His voice had dropped so low, she wasn't sure she'd heard. What she *was* sure of was that his grip on her hand was warm, and immensely comforting, and in some subtle way that she did not choose to question, it was what she wanted for the moment. In the morning she would wish she hadn't let him bridge the distance between them, but . . . this was now, and a strange harmony had woven them together, for this small span of time . . . here, with the fire beginning to die, and the silence grown so large it was *challenging* all at once.

"Hadn't we—better go back?" Saying it, her voice trembled so revealingly, she withdrew her hand in panic.

"If that's what you want," he answered, leaving it to her.

"Yes." But she did not move, though he started rising to his feet. Waiting. A moment and she detected laughter in his tone at her delay. "Take your time," he said lightly, "I wouldn't want you to make any hasty decision you'd be sorry for later."

Mocking her. He *knew*, and was amused by her ambivalence. She sat very still, eyes shut, feeling his gaze on her, conscious of a wild desire to punish him; yet conscious of something else—a craving, painful as hunger, to prolong this moment, this setting, this closeness, this night, forever and ever.

"Hell!" he swore abruptly. Then he was on the ground with her, and she in his arms, body calling to body with frightening urgency, her lips charring beneath his, and such a weakness spreading through her, she was incapable of resistance. She felt the wide spread of his hands at her back, warm, unbending as steel, crushing her close, and closer still; the hardness of his body seeking out each soft curve and hollow of her own. Half fainting, she followed the flaming journey of his hand moving upon her until it lay supine on her breast. His lips had found her throat; she could feel their warm, moist pressure quivering with his heightening passion. Slowly, deftly, his fingers began parting her blouse to trace the fullness of her breast. When his mouth moved upon it, the surge of her body wrenched from him a long-drawn groan.

"You're so beautiful," he whispered. "Val, oh, Val—I want you. And you want me, too—you know that, don't you? Don't you?" And when she did not respond, he went on. "It's no secret, Val. My body's crying for it. Yours too. We want each other, Val. We're going to have each other— and nothing that went before is going to count, Val, nothing. Not him, not anyone . . ."

His mistake, he must have known later, was in opening his mouth for any purpose other than to kiss her. And bringing in what "went before" to shatter the spell that bound them so closely, so briefly, was nothing short of stupid, he also had to acknowledge.

It brought a moment's freeze, and then Val struggled free, murmuring, "Oh, what am I *doing?*"

"It's all right," he whispered frantically.

"No. It's crazy—it's unreal—it's not me."

"Val," reaching for her shoulders to shake her gently, "Val, listen to me."

"I've already listened too much. I—don't know what got into me. This place. It's like—it robs your senses."

"Val, *think* a minute! What's back there for you? A guy you're beginning to wonder about, right? A guy with so many counts against him you need a scoreboard. Val—"

She was angry. "I'll handle that. That's *my* life, Nick. Okay? This has been—" She waved her hand dismissing what had just happened. "An illusion," she said. "Nothing more. You don't just sleep with a man because he builds a great bonfire!"

"No!" he roared, suddenly raging. "Not unless he builds one inside you. And lady, don't tell me you're not blazing like a four-alarmer right this minute. I've had women in my arms before—"

"I don't doubt that! Not for a second!" she flared, on her feet. Then she snapped, "We'd better go! This was the worst thing I ever let myself in for!"

They did not speak again until he eased the car through the gap in the cliff wall. Then she added, though stiffly, "I'm not saying it was your fault. I was equally to blame."

"Think nothing of it," he shot back. "All part of the service. Brings the customers back every time."

Chapter Eleven

SHE SLEPT THAT night in Patty's cabin, having swept a bunk clear of suitcases full of Patty's belongings. Nick's bed would have been unthinkable after the canyon incident. They were barely acknowledging each other's existence, anyway, and whatever exchange there was, of necessity, was cool and crisp. Even when they had stopped to pick up her bags from the Jaguar, his muttered, "You didn't bring much," brought a clipped response, "It was no vacation trip. Anyway, it's the children I'm bothered about. They'll run out if I can't wash for them."

"Millie'll do it. She's glad of the money and it's no strain even in that ancient washing machine. I'll tell Ruby when she comes."

Valerie refrained from saying, "She won't like that." But she had no wish to open that prickly avenue again on top of everything else. Her mind was in turmoil enough. And there was still Patty's sullenness to deal with.

Patty had gone beyond sullenness when they arrived. She had handled the children well, or they had handled her, hard to tell which. But they had finished a meal of sorts that she had been driven to prepare, and she met them at the car outraged.

111

"You took long enough! What were you doing?"

Valerie ignored her for a moment as the children came to claim their Indian headdresses. Having fitted them on and watched the youngsters go whooping off, she filled Patty in briefly on Barry's plans.

"So you can drive back with us—"

"Darned if I will!"

"Or fly back home!" Her teeth were on edge.

"Not if I can help it!"

"Or take a leap into the middle of Great Salt Lake! Darn it, Patty, I've had enough!"

"What do you think I've had! I wish people would stop deciding things for me!" Patty exploded. "Do you realize I'll be eighteen next week? And I can do whatever I please!"

"Not around here, you can't!" Nick growled, hoisting the bags from his car. "Right now, make yourself useful. Pick up one of these and head for the cabin! Come on, snap to it!"

In tears, Patty fled to the shadows rimming the clearing.

"You've been rough on her," Val murmured, following after him with the smaller bags.

"Nobody's been rough *enough* on her. The time's coming when whoever brought her up will wish they could erase the whole job and start all over!"

That time, Valerie knew, had long passed. And yet, she felt an unexpected sadness for her cousin. Obviously it was not *love* Patty felt for Nick, any more than it had been love those scores of times before for those many different boys. It was not the all-consuming fire that Val had known for Barry. It simply was not real.

And yet . . . if one really *believed* it was , then wasn't it? For a time, at least, until something happened to change it . . . ?

Here her thoughts fragmented, scattering like shards of glass in a dozen directions. She felt shaken, and when Nick broke in to inquire coolly if she'd like some supper, her eyes swung to his a moment, frightened! And she answered, just as coolly. "Maybe later, I don't know."

"Well, for crying out loud, make up your mind! Don't go prima donna on me just because of certain events!"

He spun around and strode off, and for a few awful moments, staring at his broad receding shoulders was terrifying; like plunging down, down in an elevator gone wild!

She had a crazy urge to run after him and say, "I'm sorry." But she would do no such thing. He should have known she was tired, upset. The canyon "thing" had been as hard on her as on him. He should have reasoned that she regretted bitterly what had passed between them. Yet in spite of her halfway apology for being partially to blame, the truth was *he* had instigated it. He had known precisely what he was doing, building that fire along the trail, in the evening hush. And slipping his woolen shirt around her, and humming that haunting air he'd picked up from Ruby. And all the talk about "not making sense," then seizing her, kissing her, *as if that made sense?* It was all planned. Blue-printed. What was he trying to prove, *knowing* that Barry was coming in a matter of days? And on second thought, why the devil should she say she was sorry about any of it! On the contrary, she was glad at least she'd put a stop to the thing before it ended Lord knew where and left her in *that* kettle of fish! Oh, wouldn't he have enjoyed *that* when Barry finally came. And so, the devil with him, and as for facing him across the table now, Val thought she'd rather go hungry.

Though that wasn't necessary after all. It was a foregone conclusion that among the rat's nest of Patty's litter, which Val had to sort out before she could prepare bunks for the children and herself, she would turn up some food. And she did; a half-consumed package of buns, and a third of a jar of peanut butter. Not much by way of supper, but she wasn't very hungry. And besides, it was better than crow.

If she could have stretched it out for their breakfast next morning, she would have been more than happy not to have to cross paths with Nick again, ever, for the rest of their enforced stay. But with the children and their needs, and Patty grumbling from the first opening of her eyes—about her eighteenth birthday and how she might as well be dead as the way she was—Valerie steeled herself for what could not be avoided. When the children were washed and dressed, she wandered with them to Nick's cabin.

Very early she'd heard Sunny come galloping in, and very early gritted her teeth at Patty's sputtering sarcasm, "Why does she bother to go home at all?" But now, other than the horse tethered in a grassy patch, she saw no one around. The Land Rover? That, too, was gone. She wondered, but then they were at the cabin door, the children in their feathered headgear mounting an attack with a roar and a bellow.

It seemed empty within. Then with startling suddenness, Ruby emerged from the shadow.

"Oh, I thought Nick was here," Val said uncomfortably.

There came a strained pause. Even the children were quiet. Val had to ask, "Where is he?" if only to get some response.

"He's gone."

"Gone?"

"He took his cameras up the trail. He won't be back all day."

"Oh?"

"I'm straightening up his things," she volunteered pointedly.

"Yes. I see. Well, you don't have to bother about breakfast for us."

"I wasn't going to."

Val ignored the thrust. Given a choice, she'd have left the cabin until after the girl was finished. But the children began clamoring for food and Patty had just trailed in after them, and the cabin suddenly took on the feel of an armed camp.

"I'll keep out of your way," she breathed, moving cautiously to the camp stove and the stocked "pantry" shelf.

"I'm about finished here," Ruby said. "Nick said you'll have a bundle of the children's washing for Ma."

"Oh, yes. I'll surely appreciate it. I left it on the chair

in the other cabin. Or shall I bring it to you?"

"I'll get it," Ruby said, and with a final caress of Nick's bedroll, started away—only to pause unexpectedly. "I'm meeting him up the trail. He's going to let me help him."

"Help him with what!" Patty challenged. "What do you know about cameras?"

Ruby bristled visibly, answering through clenched teeth, "I know how to keep quiet when he's working!" Relishing her small triumph, she added, "Nick happens to want my picture, too. Did he ask for one of yours?"

Patty had deserved that, Val thought; even the poisonous glare that went with it. But that same look settled briefly on her own face and for one sickening instant before the girl turned away Jake Jordan's malicious stare leaped at her from his daughter's sullen eyes.

Breakfast was a helter-skelter affair after that, which somehow Valerie managed to organize with her mind in total disarray. That look. It could not have been meant for her! The two girls had been at each other's throats well before Valerie arrived. And Val had gone out of her way not to ruffle Ruby's feathers. If the girl imagined she was trying to compete for Nick, she was well off center. Actually, how could she? She knew about Barry!

In the end, she felt sorry for Ruby. Nick was right. She had small chance of ever rising above her parents' sad level, unless she did it on her own. But if Nick thought he was helping Ruby by taking her, all willing and eager, up the trail for a photo session...he was beneath contempt!

"What are *you* so mad about?" Patty asked. "Again!"

Val's eyes leaped across the rim of her coffee mug. "What are you talking about?"

"Your hands are shaking. And your eyes look like bombs just went off. Like if you could, you wouldn't mind drowning that girl!"

"Damn it, Patty, I've had it with you and the day's only begun! You wash these dishes and I'm going to straighten up our cabin."

She didn't wait for the usual grumble. She got out of

there fast. The children waved from their stone fort where they'd flown still gulping their breakfast, and she waved back, slowing down to chat. They had a kind of warfare in progress, shooting make-believe arrows and screaming hilariously as each enemy bit the dust. Val had to smile. They were so realistic at play. "Don't shoot me, don't shoot me!" she cried in mock alarm, scurrying across their no-man's-land.

"Aw, we wouldn't shoot you, we're only shooting baddies," Gillian volunteered, and Peter, loosing an "arrow" shouted to the skies, "Got him! There goes Daddy. *I just killed him!*"

Val froze. She stared at the boy, her icy hands groping at her face.

"Darling," she murmured at length, "you didn't mean that—"

"Sure."

"No, Peter, you didn't. You don't mean you 'killed' your daddy. Don't say that, dear. Not even in fun. It's pretty awful."

"Why's it awful?" he challenged, his face darkening in the way she'd come to dread. "He almost killed Mommy—"

"Oh, no, Peter, please—" Her face twisted in pain and annoyance, something she'd never felt for the children before.

"He did and I hate him—"

"Me, too," Gillian picked up. "We're going to chop him up and cook him on the fire, that's what we'll do—"

"Children!" Val was at her wit's end. There seemed no way to reach them. She was their friend until the subject of Barry arose. Then every time they blocked her out. Now she backed off, admitting her own helplessness, and left them to their fiendish whims. As she continued to the cabin, crestfallen, she vowed once again that things were going to change, must change. And Barry was going to change with it, once they were together again.

She was a short distance from the cabin when Ruby

appeared abruptly in its doorway, the small laundry bundle slung across her shoulder. She shot Valerie a glance, then, seeming to hesitate, moved hastily to where the horse was tethered. Valerie thought it odd that she would deliberately take the long way around simply to avoid passing her. Just as she thought it most odd that the girl had taken nearly half an hour simply to pick up the laundry bundle which had been readied for her. But neither of these strange moves struck her with such shattering impact as her discovery moments later in the cabin.

Chapter Twelve

THE FLOOR-LENGTH PATCHWORK SKIRT, a favorite, lay in a heap as if hastily dropped. Val had not left it out in the open. Actually, it had been folded near the bottom of her suitcase. She had not had the need to wear it, and at one point had wondered why she had bothered to bring it.

Thoroughly baffled, she scooped it off the floor, frankly irritated with the girl for poking around among her belongings. She threw back the lid of her suitcase and, yes, everything that had been neatly folded was jammed in any which way. Annoyed, she shook the skirt out to start folding it back in shape—then abruptly gasped.

From the waistband to the hem, *there was a great long tear!*

She stared, incredulous! Suddenly she was shaking. The look! Jake Jordan's malevolence in his daughter's eyes! It *had* been for her! And now this! Why would she take out her hatred for Patty on herself? And in such a despicable way! What was she trying to tell Val, leaving that ripped-apart skirt out where she would see it? Was it some kind of a warning?

And what would Nick say to that? Oh, she knew what he'd say. She knew it so surely, she'd only be wasting her time showing it to him. He'd say, "Sure you didn't rip it yourself?"

118

"Well, darn! I never saw such a hell-hole!" she fumed, dumping everything from the suitcase to fold it carefully back before Patty could show up. *She* didn't have to know about this, either, Val decided. Nothing else had been damaged, but she supposed the girl just hadn't gotten around to it. That was why she had beat such a hurried retreat when she saw Val approaching.

"Well, good luck to her! And to Nick, too, with his pious talk about *h-helping* her! They deserve each other."

And this was the man who had such cutting things to say about Barry! Her eyes stung and she rubbed her lids savagely. The next time he had any snide cracks to make about Barry, he was going to hear a few things about *his* choice of a love! How bitterly she regretted now that scene on the trail the night before! That she had let him get that far with her! But . . . maybe it had to happen, if only to point up to her how decent Barry was by contrast.

How could she have been so upset over that Ivy Ashley nonsense? When they were married, *she* would handle Ivy as only a woman can under such sticky circumstances. If Ivy wanted to go to sleep in their bed with her shoes on, and her sunglasses, and even an umbrella for all she cared, Val would personally volunteer to sit beside her and hold her hand!

The day dragged on, the heat mounting until at midday the whole world seemed aflame. To her relief, Patty decided on a siesta in the cabin before lunch. She had worn herself out grumping about all morning, her pet gripe relating now to her advancing years. "Eighteen in a week. I feel—decayed. My life's so empty . . ."

Val had comforted her with the reminder that the ratio of men to girls in New York was so much more satisfying.

"There's only one man for me and you know it!" she had retorted.

"Oh, yes, yes. I recall hearing that about a whole string of your swains, darling. Now, off with you. I'll take the children for a ramble."

"In this heat?"

"The canyon floors aren't bad. If there's any breeze, it'll be there up the trail a bit."

"And so will you-know-who, coming back without you-know-who-else!"

"Patty," she exploded finally, "the mood I am in with this whole setup out here, you darn well know who had better be getting on with her siesta!"

Then she left her, to join the only happy creatures around.

"Hi, kids!" she called coming up behind them. She was greeted with a storm of "arrows."

"Whang! Whang! Whang! Why don't you fall down?" Peter shouted. "You're dead!"

"I know." She laughed. "Wouldn't you rather take out the old peace pipe and walk with me along the trail?"

"No."

"Ah, why not? I'd love some company."

"We mustn't. Nick told us not to. There's the old mine—"

"We're not going that-a-way, pardner."

"And there's snakes."

"I don't see any snakes."

"Nick says you don't till it's too late."

Val sighed. She couldn't argue with sound advice to the children. And it did keep them from wandering. She only marveled at their obedience. But then, they were so free and happy here. For the first time she wondered if they would leave without a scene. But then there'd be the rambling trip home, with stops at interesting places. If only she could tell them about it, prepare them, win them over to anticipating the homebound journey with their father with any degree of excitement...

Impossible. The least mention of his name blackened their moods. And hers, consequently.

She forfeited her walk, not wishing to leave them alone, and retreated to Nick's cabin, having better sense than to retreat to Patty's. Here it was cooler and she could watch the children through the open door. Here, too, was a thing she had been curious about since the night of the music.

She had noticed a stack of paper, scored for transcribing,

upon a rough shelf. She felt no hesitation in bringing the pile carefully down to the table. Nick had hardly been secretive about it.

Valerie knew little enough about music from the professional slant, but she could follow a melody in her head when it was laid before her in note form. And as she scanned Nick's neatly inked characters, she found herself softly humming the tunes, the very ones he had piped in the night. And more, those she had heard from Ruby's own lips the morning after.

They were haunting and plaintive and lonely, and some had words above the scores that she recognized from folk songs she had heard before, with variations that were clearly regional.

And then she came upon one melody that abruptly robbed her breath. As she picked up the air, her pulses throbbed again with recognition . . . beside the fire, the night before . . . the song without words.

She turned it face down, impulsively, as if to block out memory. Which it did not; in fact it was a rash and foolish move. For there was writing on the back—words no doubt that Nick had finally found, sometime in the night?

She read them over guardedly and was startled to find them familiar. But, of course, she thought after a quick mental scramble. She had placed them, as would any English major, perhaps, who had happened among other things to have written her college thesis on Robert Louis Stevenson! It was the last of three verses she recalled, and it came back easily now . . . until suddenly it sent such a stab of pain through her, she nearly abandoned it. But she read it all the same:

And this shall be for music, when no one else is
    near,
The fine song for singing, the rare song to hear!
That only I remember, that only you admire.
Of the broad road that stretches and the roadside
    fire.

She arrived at the end, only to begin again, whispering it this time, slowly, with long meaningful pauses between phrases. Her breath came hard, and harder. Incredibly, the inked words started blurring. Her voice stumbled, and choked off. Abruptly her hands flew to her face, stemming the tears at their source. *What in heaven's name was wrong with her?* What was it that suddenly demanded to be faced? Why did it matter so much, at this moment, that he was off somewhere with Ruby? For a ghastly instant, she denied hotly to herself that it mattered at all. But in the next breath, she knew she lied. She knew *it mattered!* Knew there was something she wanted, desperately. His arms enfolding her? His body? Oh, more than *that*. Something beyond defining. Something she had not known existed, and not knowing, had not yearned for. Yet having met it, she wanted it with an all-consuming hunger.

Ask it of Barry, her conscience commanded. But no, Barry, for all he had to offer, did not have *that*. With Barry, things *moved*. Whirlwinds. Earthquakes. Tidal waves that caught her up and swept her along in his wake.

Nick? Nick was a whole different thing. Nick moved like a broad and lordly river. Peaceful. For all their constant wrangling, she could feel that in him. Here before her—his work—lay the proof. Stacks of it, quietly accumulated over weeks, months, possibly years. Work that could well bring him recognition, scholarly notice, but hardly wealth. Perhaps little more than the satisfying pleasure of having finished a task he had set himself.

Barry, the organizer, ever alert to opportunity, with an uncanny talent for cultivating the key people to open doors or help him up the ladder—Ivy flew to mind but was speedily thrust out, leaving a dark stain to be dealt with another time—Barry surely would end up a wealthy, influential man.

This would never be Nick's lot. Val knew that with the same intuition that told her Nick could not care less. Where Barry stormed through life, Nick slogged along, taking time to see, to feel, to discover, to hold, to know, to understand.

Nick took time even to lean down, grasp a hand, and help someone up beside him. Barry—*not* unkind, oh, never that; he was not *unkind*, he was just so *busy*—Barry, seeing a need, would assign someone to do it for him. He would never turn his back, or ignore a need, she emphasized to herself guiltily. He would see that it was handled, by someone, and go on with what he was doing.

And—well, what was wrong with that, she thought defensively. What was wrong with Barry wanting to get ahead in this world? Why all at once had she begun to pick flaws? Hadn't she known him, lived with him long enough to be aware of the finicky little things in others one has to put up with if one is not to live life alone? She knew Barry's quirks, and she was not perfect herself. And heaven knew, she and Nick were at each other's throats all the time, and there was nothing, really *nothing* between them. There never had been anything.

For a crazy instant, her eyes flooded again, but she wiped them angrily. She loved *Barry*. She *loved* him. This thing with Nick was an aberration that had seized upon her the moment she entered the canyon. It had been like entering a dream where all things became distorted, and all perspectives took on strange dimensions. She would be free of it only when she left Jordan's Hole, which could not be too soon. Then, and only then, her world would settle back on its familiar foundation. Barry would be there beside her, blowing up hurricanes, to be sure, and if she remembered Nick at all, eventually, it would be rarely, and only if she stumbled by chance across that verse sometime, or caught a snatch of song... And if it happened, she would laugh and remember this moment, *now*, and wonder how she could ever have been, even briefly, as silly and man-crazy as teenaged Patty Linwood.

Quietly after a time, she stacked the papers and placed them on their high shelf. When she walked out into the sunlight, she felt wooden, drained of all emotion.

Leaning in the doorway, grasping reality once more, she saw the Land Rover rounding the bend from the trail. He was at the wheel, alone. If there'd been a place to run and hide, she would have fled to it. As it was, she was still there, transfixed, when he unloaded his camera equipment and carried it through.

She said nothing as he brushed past her, because nothing would come. Nor did he seem to expect it. He scarcely glanced her way, though he did remark, "Mailed another note to Doug Ledyard. Told him to speed it up if he could."

She took a deep breath and controlled her voice with difficulty. "Thank you. He couldn't possibly get here too soon."

"Amen, sister!" he agreed, biting the words short. "And a hundred years from now, we'll have forgotten the whole thing."

"It'll hardly take me that long," she retorted, walking away stiffly. How right she had been. She felt *nothing* for him, he merely irritated her.

"Tell me about it in a hundred years," he called after her ramrod back.

If he meant it was going to take her a century to forget this place, this time, she did not know, she did not want to think. She had a premonition that the waiting days ahead would be rough enough as it was. And near the close of the third day, she knew she had underestimated. The atmosphere had gone electric with friction, the only thing agreed upon by all being the wisdom of avoiding one another.

Except for the need to use the camp stove, Val would not have gone near Nick's cabin. As it was, he was considerate enough to absent himself when the mealtime hours arrived, even declining to have her cook for him along with the others.

"Ruby'll see to it," he told her curtly the first time she offered, and she fell back with a crazy hurt.

Ruby did indeed, with relish! Ruby was there so early and so late that when Patty muttered, "She's there all night if you ask me!" She was merely reflecting Val's own suspicions.

The girl was being quite artful at avoiding Val, too. And

well she might, Val thought angrily that third day, seating herself on a rock in the open to stitch up the rent in the patchwork skirt. It was not the deftest of mending jobs. But she was not in the best of moods, either. Jake had brought in the water drums earlier and had been quite cozy with Nick and Ruby over coffee in the cabin. When he'd rolled a drum to the rear of the girls' shack, he'd remarked as he straightened up to leave. "Reckon that ought to be the last of 'em, eh? 'Fore long, it'll be gettin' too hot for you around here."

In spite of his sweeping look up at the sun, she was in a mood to take his remark as a direct threat. It had angered her so, she had gone straightway for her skirt and emergency needle and thread, and planted herself where no one could fail to see her.

Ruby had seen. Coming out of Nick's cabin after Jake departed, Nick right behind her, she had seen and pulled up short an instant. For a split second, Valerie's eyes had seized hers and held. The girl was shaken, no doubt of it. But it was Nick who inadvertently saved her day.

"Well, well, she sews a fine seam," he rumbled, biting down hard on his pipe stem. "Satan's having one devil of a time finding idle hands around here for mischief-making!"

Val swung her glare his way. "Satan's done his miserable best around here already! Take my word for it!"

Ruby's face seemed expressionless. Nick's eyes glinted amusement. "There, there, you'll prick a finger, love!" he cautioned.

Val leaped to her feet, ready to thrust the skirt under their noses and pour out precisely what had been done.

But in that instant a motor came roaring around the bend, and nothing, for any of them, was ever to be the same again.

Chapter Thirteen

STILL BLINDED WITH RAGE, Val saw a dusty Jeep jouncing into the clearing. Her throat felt so thick with tears she wanted to escape. "Hey-y" Nick shouted. "Doug, good show, fella! You came on the double!"

A lanky, sandy-haired young man unfurled a pair of long, muscular legs from beneath the wheel and stretched them one after the other to the ground. Val thought all the dust that had not settled on the Jeep had blanketed him instead, except where a pair of brilliant blue eyes peered out under his bristly blond brows.

"Man, I know an SOS when I hear one!" he said, thrusting a huge bony paw into Nick's hand and shaking hard. "Got your note late yesterday. Couldn't let the old prof down! Got your fanbelt, too."

"It's not mine, it's hers," Nick said, turning to introduce Valerie. "She broke down, right outside my trail, conveniently."

"I saw it," Doug said.

Val managed a smile for him, submerging a killing stare at Nick. "I can't thank you enough," she told the young man, offering her hand.

As he took it, he glanced over at Nick with a gallant,

if blunt observation. "You've got to be out of your head, man. What was the panic?"

Val laughed. "I was supposed to be on a whirlwind trip here and back. To pick up my cousin—"

"Who also managed," Nick put in unasked, "to get herself stranded here, conveniently."

"Wow, how do you do it, Prof? Why don't *I* ever get that lucky?" His glance had moved to Ruby, who'd drawn back behind Nick.

"Nope, wrong girl," Nick corrected. "This is Ruby Jordan from the general store up the trail. Valerie's cousin is sulking in their cabin where she has spent the last week. It's her stock in trade. Sometimes she doesn't show up except to eat, which she does quite well, regardless."

Doug laughed, then added, "I'm gritty. How's chances for a tub?"

"A tub? Fella, which Hilton did you stay at last?"

"Oh, it's all right." Ruby spoke up for the first time, shyly. "Not a tub, I mean. But there's water enough. And Pa can run over an extra drum tomorrow, Nick. I'll show Doug where—"

Ledyard grinned, his brows shooting up and down in a mock leer. "Hey, how about that? You don't get *that* at any Hilton!"

Ruby flushed a beet red. "I mean, I'll take you there, and . . ."

"I know, I know. I get to scrub my own magnificent biceps with no help from the fair maiden." He sighed.

Ruby, laughing, led the way. "See you all," Doug called, following after.

Nick met Val's look absently and began knocking the ashes from his pipe. He was smiling—oddly, she thought.

"Well," he said at length, "I must've done her some good. The girl's come a long way."

She studied him a moment. "You mean that takes care of your sticky problem? Man stuck with girl. New man arrives. Girl becomes unstuck. Hooray!"

His eyes flickered with a cold light. "And that's all you

can read into what I just said, is it? Well, if you knew how
shy she was when I got here, so she'd hide before she'd
show herself to strangers—hell, even Doug didn't see her
the first time he came through with me—you'd understand
how far she's come."

"Yes? Perhaps. But from my experience with her," she
added, clutching the half-mended skirt hard against her,
"she still has a long way to go!"

"Whatever that means," he growled. "Anyway, Doug
and I will get that fanbelt on for you without delay. Is after
dinner early enough?"

"You *know* I have to wait for Barry."

"Yes, that's a nuisance! Well—bear with us, we'll bear
with you!" He started away, then swung around briefly.
"For tonight, we'll all eat together. Tell the princess if she
gives me a hard time, she'll stand up all the way back East.
And you—see if you can't do something about that shade
of bilious green you turn whenever Ruby's around. Barry's
liable to notice when he comes, and call it jealousy!"

She was so close to tears when she reached her cabin,
had Patty realized, she might not have chosen that moment
to whine, "If you think I'm going to eat with her at the
table, think again."

"You'll eat when and with whom I tell you to, Patty
Linwood—or you'll stand up all the way back home!"

"What're *you* so rattled about? Oh, don't answer that,
I know. Every time you see those two together, you're
worse than I am!"

Val's fists clenched. "More nonsense! Listen, there's
company for dinner, the fellow who brought my fanbelt—"

"Cheers!" she began, then, "What fellow?"

"Nick's friend. Doug Ledyard. And if you make trouble
in front of him—"

"*I* never make trouble! People do it to *me*! Nick's been
downright nasty to me ever since you came."

"All right! Maybe if you act human, he'll be a real doll
tonight. You just might have him all to yourself! He might
even suggest eloping with you!" Her voice was rising. She

had passed the peak of restraint. "Ruby has her eye on Doug, which leaves you a clear field!"

A hush filled the cabin all at once. Val rubbed her aching head and longed to lie down.

"A clear field?" Patty murmured. "What about you?"

"I won't answer such a stupid question. You see me going mad waiting for Barry so we can clear out of this lunatic asylum and *you* ask—"

"All right," Patty breathed, her eyes glowing. "I just wanted to be sure. Now! Watch out, Nick McKenzie. Here I come!"

Valerie gave up. What was the point of bucking that kind of bullheaded determination any longer? Let the gods cope with it, those whose job it was to handle rotten kids!

She'd have given much to skip dinner herself this night! But with the children and Patty to keep in line, to say nothing of what Nick would make of it, she could hardly plead a headache.

The youngsters came at her call for a wash-up— large-eyed and openly suspicious.

"Why's everybody so excited?" Peter asked, "And who's the man with the Jeep?"

"He's a friend of Nick's, dear, and he's brought the new fanbelt for our Jag," Val explained, careful to suppress even the faintest hint of relief. With the children, she knew now she walked on thin ice.

"Does that mean we've got to go now?" Gillian asked, her eyes firm on Val's face. There was no evading it.

"Well, yes. That is, as soon as your Daddy comes."

"Aw-w," she said, but Peter said nothing, and for the first time Val wished he'd yell some protest, scream, throw himself about and make a scene. Anything would be better than the droop of his face and the gleam of a tear in his eye.

"Peter," she said softly, but he swung around and followed his sister to the wash basin, wanting none of her comfort.

Val, fighting off depression, left her own freshening up

until the others were finished. But when she and the children were ready to leave, Patty, still in a terry robe, hair newly washed, was burrowing among Val's things.

"What on earth are you doing?"

"Borrowing your dirndl skirt, the one with the daisies."

"Without even asking? What's wrong with a pair of clean jeans?"

"I'm changing tactics. I have a feeling Nick goes for the sweet country-girl type."

"Sweet country girls don't throw themselves at men who don't want them."

"What does he know? Ah, here!" She whipped the daisy skirt from Val's case, upsetting everything else in it. "Just right. And may I borrow your peasant blouse? Of course, Patty dear, help yourself."

Val threw up her hands in resignation and started away. "Dinner's in about ten minutes. At least have the decency to be on time!"

Predictably enough, Patty had not yet arrived when the others were ready to sit down. Nick had the cabin ablaze with candles and the warm glow, for the time at least, seemed to feather out the edginess among them. Ruby, her red hair making firelight of its own, still avoided Valerie's eyes. But then Val's eyes, busily avoiding Nick's, had settled approvingly on Doug Ledyard.

The young man glowed from his scrubbing. He had shaved, and in fresh denims he was about the pleasantest and most refreshing person Val had yet seen at this benighted hole. He'd taken at once to the children and seated them beside his place. Valerie expected a sour look from Ruby over that arrangement, but it did not come. Ruby took the foot of the table which Val would have preferred for herself. That left her a vacancy at Nick's right hand, or one at Ruby's—between the Devil and the Deep, she thought, uncertain which to choose. Nick settled it with a brusque, "Here, Valerie," holding the seat at his side.

"Where's the princess?"

"She'll come along any minute," Val murmured.

Doug said, "Oh, shouldn't we wait?"

"Over my dead body! Nick muttered. "Ruby worked hard on this meal. It's good and hot and ready. *Her* hard luck if there's none left when she decides to show up!"

It was, Val had to agree, a splendid corned-beef hash— no mean task on the small camp stove. Ruby had also managed a kind of cornmeal fritter, rich and tasty enough to bring a small cry of pleasure from Val before she realized.

"These are *good*, Ruby. You're a fine cook!"

The girl glanced up, and even in the candle glow, her dark flush was obvious. She seemed almost to squirm and Val was regretting her impulsive compliment when Nick's head flung up and attention was thankfully diverted. For there stood Patty in the open door.

For a fleeting second, Val almost admired her for the transformation she had effected. But knowing it was as phony as a three-dollar bill, it was hardly worth dwelling on.

"*Your Majesty!*" Nick growled.

"Oh, Nick, I'm so sorry to be late. Forgive me," she purred. "I had to wait to the last at the wash basin."

Val gasped. Patty got no further because Doug Ledyard's chair scraped back and, gentlemen that he was, he rose. Nick did not follow suit.

"Sit down, Doug," he muttered. "The princess isn't used to that kind of treatment around here. Liable to spoil her."

Doug either did not hear or chose to remain standing. Patty, too, stood her place letting a slow smile light her face. It was quite a face, too, Val had to concede. Her newly washed hair formed a shimmering aura about the perfect heart shape. Her lips remained parted and moist, and her wide purple eyes stared back at Doug as if it were the first time in all her tender years that she had ever *seen* a man.

Val suppressed a distinct impulse to tell her, "Cool it, Ruby saw him first," even though she knew perfectly well this was part of Patty's announced change of tactics. She would divert all her attention to the only other male present, expecting to drive Nick mad with jealousy. At that moment, apparently, it had not yet begun to work, for he broke in impatiently.

"Okay, sit down, so the rest of us can get on with Ruby's feast."

Doug had walked around to pull out Patty's seat—a packing case in this instance—and the girl seemed to float across the space, her eyes barely leaving Ledyard.

What an actress, Val thought with disgust.

All through the meal, Patty was silent, her eyes mostly on her plate. When she looked up at all, it was with a shy smile across at Doug. Only once did Val catch her wide-eyed glance at Nick, a look utterly devoid of coyness. Val thought she was really overdoing it, but at least she wasn't causing trouble. One had to be grateful for small blessings.

Dinner over, Valerie offered to wash the dishes, but Ruby declined her help. "No, thank you."

"But don't you want to go outside? With Doug?"

Ruby flashed her a glance. Then turning her back to clear the table, said, "Why should I?"

"I just thought—" Val began, then lost patience with her, too, and wandered out with the others.

Nick, lighting his pipe on a bench beside the cabin, barely looked her way. She was intensely aware of him, but scarcely grazed him with her eyes. Off in the shadows near the cliff wall, Patty and Doug, a demure arm's length apart, strolled together. Val's head reeled with the new tangle of emotions this girl was managing to set off with her act, while leading young Ledyard a false and merry chase! Patty was without conscience. But what really irritated Val was that the fraud being pulled on Nick was having its effect. Certainly, she noted in a surreptitious sidelong glance, his eyes were clearly slanted on Patty and Doug. With a fillip of laughter, a perverse devil in her spoke.

"Well! How does it feel facing up to the first competition you've had to contend with in your 'secluded rendezvous'? How our blessings do brighten as they take their leave."

He bit down on his pipe and without a second's pause

answered from the corner of his mouth, "How our hackles do rise at the yawl of a *cat!*"

"Oh, for heaven's sake?" she muttered and left him, his low chuckle trailing her. So all right, she had asked for it. But it was true. Jealousy was oozing all over him!

Suddenly, the thought of several more days in this love-hate atmosphere before she could hope for Barry's arrival grew so appalling she marched straightway to the cabin and began readying the youngsters for bed. The riot act she had prepared for Patty would have to wait until morning. Her head truly ached now, and not too long after Peter and Gillian drifted off, she curled up in her own bedroll to make it an early night.

The last thing she heard before she slept was Ruby's horse clippety-clopping off in the moonlight. And the first thing at the crack of dawn, Ruby's horse returning.

From a hazy distance another sound intruded, the hum of a motor cutting off abruptly at almost the same moment that Sunny's hoofbeats halted nearby. Val turned over, trying for sleep again, only to bolt awake at a loud rap on the door. Springing to her feet, she snatched up her robe and struggled into it. Thankfully, neither Patty nor the children stirred.

At the door, she opened a crack to peer out. "Ruby!"

"Your man's here!" The girl started backing off almost as she said it.

"B-Barry, here? *Already!*" Val gasped.

"Over there," Ruby added with a toss of her head over her shoulder as she turned to lead Sunny away for tethering.

Too stunned and excited to dress, Val closed the door softly behind her and started racing across the clearing. She could not believe how quickly he had come, and with what perfect timing. But there, nonetheless, loomed a car in the early mists. And there, as her eyes clawed the gray dawn vapors, she picked out the figure at the wheel.

She laughed, closing the distance, imagining Barry laughing, too, at the sight of her, her tangled hair flying, dashing barefoot across the stony soil to meet him. Yards

away, the deceptive haze suddenly parted—and she stopped
dead in her tracks.

A man lounged in the seat, watching her. A stranger
with chilly eyes.

Chapter Fourteen

"WH-WHO—ARE YOU?" she whispered, the sharpness of her disappointment numbed by his open hostility.

He was slow to answer. But when he did, it was swift and crushing. "I'm Gregory Drummond. Claire's brother."

It was a knife, straight to her heart. Then he twisted it. "I assume you have heard of Claire?"

"Claire—" she breathed. "Yes."

"Yes," he echoed. "Lots of Barry's women have."

She reeled, but this time in anger. "I happen *not* to be— one of 'Barry's women'!"

He hadn't expected such a response. His surprise showed in his momentary pause, which she hastened to fill. "I happen to be the woman your sister *stole* him from! The woman who was there before Claire ever knew he existed."

He had not expected that, either. Clearly he had never even heard of her. "Oh?"

"Oh. I'm sure she wouldn't have told you *that!*"

His brows arched. He answered obliquely, "Obviously, you don't know Claire." And as she struggled to frame a reply, added, "Nor Barry, either."

"I'm the best judge of that!" she snapped. Then, fury mounting, "How did you find me, anyway? What are you doing here?"

"I've come for the children!"

"The chil—*you're mad!* What on earth? Do you think I'd just hand them over to you, a stranger? They're Barry's!"

"And Claire's," he reminded her, unruffled.

"But they're his for this month! The court gave him visiting rights!"

"And he's making the most of his time with them, isn't he?" He spoke softly, in sharp contrast to Val's spiraling tones. Abruptly he opened his car door. "Mind if I stretch my legs? I've been driving all night from Phoenix, using the route you sent Barry!"

He stepped to the ground, a man of medium height and build, graying slightly at the temples. His eyes at closer range were warmer, pleasanter than she was prepared to admit.

"Where *is* Barry?" she asked suspiciously. Why would Barry have volunteered that route? What had that powerful Drummond clan done to him this time? "Is he in Phoenix?"

"He was in New York yesterday."

"But he was due in Phoenix about now."

"I wouldn't know, Miss Sheppard. That wasn't my affair."

"What was?"

"I told you. Claire needs the children."

"Claire *needs?*" She scoffed openly. "Explain that, please! I mean, forgive my denseness, but it's hard to understand Claire's need of Peter and Gillian while she's flitting around all the fashionable spots in Europe."

"She is?" His voice hardened, and his eyes narrowed slowly. "There are a few little facts, Miss Sheppard, that have come to you rather distorted. Unsurprisingly, I might add."

"Meaning, I suppose, Barry has lied to me? No, Mr. Drummond. My information comes from other sources. Newspaper columns, for instance."

His smile came slowly, almost pityingly, she thought, bridling. "Gossip columns. All those neat little planted items that people imbibe religiously with their morning coffee! Well, as a member of the Drummond family, I'm happy to see *somebody* on our payroll is minding our store!" His tone went harsh again. "Do you imagine for one minute we'd like it breezed all over the lot that Claire Drummond has been in and out of psychiatric care for at least five of her seven years of marriage to that—that—" He broke off so emotionally, Valerie flinched.

She could not believe it. She would not accept it. She felt a thunderous roaring in her head, his voice weaving in and out.

"Claire is in Switzerland under therapy. Again! She was flown there near collapse. That's why we had to step up the children's visit to their father. Now her psychiatrist insists the children be nearby. We've taken a chalet on a slope close to the sanitarium, and I'm flying them over just as quickly as I can pick them up. Have I made myself clear?"

Her hand found her throat that was thick with pain and shock. And yet—she grasped like a drowning person at a single straw that mercifully floated in reach. "How do I know you're not making it all up?"

"I'm glad you thought of that," he muttered. "I almost forgot Barry's letter." He reached into his jacket and brought out an envelope. Her hand trembled, taking it from him. She hesitated, her eyes stinging. "Go ahead, read it."

"Later," she murmured. She could not, in his presence, no matter what Barry had to say. She asked instead, "What if the children won't go with you? They've grown—" Here her voice choked without warning, and she dashed a tear furiously from her lids. He waited. "They've grown very close, very dear; I love them."

"I believe you," he said quietly, "but so do we."

For the briefest space their eyes met, drained of hostility.

"As for their going with me—when they wake up, tell them Uncle Greg's here." He spoke softly. "You'll have your answer."

She turned away, clutching Barry's letter. And the first thing she saw was Nick approaching. She'd have given

much to evade what had to be explained. But when he came
forward, his hand outstretched to welcome "Barry," evasion
was impossible. She made it brief, terse. "This is the children's uncle, Gregory Drummond. They are, uh—"

He spared her. "There's been an emergency. Their
mother needs them."

"Oh, too bad," she heard Nick say gravely. "Well, come
over and have some coffee."

The rest of their conversation drifted off on the morning
air as she hurried beyond earshot, Barry's letter crinkling
in her hand, like a telegram one holds, fearful of opening,
half dreading, half knowing, staving off the moment of
confirmation.

"Dearest Val," he wrote, "Fortune smiles. We're getting
a terrific break! The kids are off our hands . . . meet me
. . . Phoenix . . . on to Las Vegas . . ." The words began
to blur, to fade. She folded the letter, then crumpled it into
a ball, without ever getting beyond those words. There was
no need.

With a valiant effort she squared her shoulders and
marched off to see if the children were awake. They were,
awake and scrambling all over Patty who for some obscure
reason was in a cheerful mood.

"Darlings!" she told them. "Guess who's come?"

There was a thick silence. Then Peter spoke, his voice
thin, "N-not—Daddy?"

She swallowed hard. "Would you settle for Uncle Greg?"

"Uncle Greg!"

Gillian on her knees in Patty's bunk began jumping up
and down until Patty yelled, "Ouch, my stomach!" Peter
had already raced wildly from the cabin in his pajamas,
shouting, "Where is he?"

When they were both gone, when Patty had leaped from
bed and ducked out back to wash—another first, Val remembered later—she went quietly about packing the children's clothes and laying out fresh ones for their journey.

Later, when it was *all* over, she realized the only tears
she'd had to shed were for them, when they were piling

into their uncle's car and suddenly begged a large last kiss—
"before we go to Mommy. *We're going to Mommy*, Val,
did Uncle Greg tell you?"

"Yes, dear."

"We're not going to Daddy." Their faces scrunched with
distaste. "Daddy's layin' out there—" Gillian pointed, and
Peter, his eyes narrow slits, added, "Yeah, with an arrow
in him!"

Two arrows, Val thought, keeping a tight rein on her
emotions as she hugged them hard. After waving them off,
she turned to find Nick's face swimming up through a warm,
salty blur.

"Have you put the new fanbelt on?" she asked huskily.

"Mind if we have breakfast first? Only the kids have
eaten, you know."

But neither of their voices was quite up to sparring
strength.

That built up later, with Patty's help after a breakfast
which Ruby had prepared. Once more, they'd all sat at table
together, Doug remarking, "Too bad the kids had to go.
They were fun."

"And we're next," Val said firmly.

"Oh, sorry about that, Valerie, honestly," Doug said
earnestly.

"Some people aren't," she murmured flicking a glance
at Nick which brushed lightly over Ruby as well. The girl
was staring into her coffee mug, wooden-faced. Nick went
on chewing a bite of sausage with no apparent interest in
the chatter. But Patty, the new Patty, Val noted, said very
softly, "Valerie, oh, I know we're going home, but it's
been so wonderful here. Can't we just stay a few days, until
my birthday?"

"You'll celebrate that with your mother. You owe it to
her."

"Valerie, *please?* I'd like so much to turn eighteen here.
It's been the biggest summer of my life."

"Sorry, you've had your fun, Patty. Now I've got to get
back to New York. Without delay."

"What in hell for *now?*" Nick's abrupt growl seemed to startle himself as much as the others. He glanced around reddening.

Val's eyes widened. "Really, I can't believe you're urging us to stay!"

He cleared his throat. "Uh, neither can I. We all go bananas sometimes. Mad McKenzie they called me on campus."

"And they will *again*, Professor!"

"Well, what I meant was—that other thing you were going back for, it's over, isn't it?"

She flushed dangerously. That he had the gall to bring it up!

"What *other thing* were you referring to?" She was bent on seeing him squirm.

"The fiancé bit, remember?"

Restraint came hard, but she managed. "You're the soul of taste, my good man. Still, it may surprise you to know—though possibly not, since you were taking it all in when I phoned New York—that I have other business to get back to. A shop to run!"

"Sounded to me as if they were getting along just dandy without you!"

" 'They' happens to be Deirdre Pennington who is a busy woman in her own right with a life of her own to lead. I can't go on imposing."

"Hell! What's a few more days until Patty's birthday?" Nick followed that with a large gulp of coffee. When he set his mug down, Valerie was studying him narrowly.

"There's something fishy about you, McKenzie. I can't believe what I'm hearing!" she said in a tone heavy with skepticism. "Would you care to—uh—thrash this out, privately, so each of us can say what we're thinking and straighten out a few misconceptions I would hate to leave behind?"

"Not with you in the mood you're in, I wouldn't," he answered. "Too much fur flying around here already. All

I say is, we've suffered each other this long, what in hell difference can a few days mean? Your problem, Val, is that you want to run the whole works. Well, we're right back where we started, and this is still my—"

"Harem?" she cut in acidly. "Not for long. You should be thanking me, Nick. I happen to know what I'm saving you from."

And Val was certain she did. The way he was eyeing Patty lately, he was going to get into deep trouble the day she turned eighteen. Val had a very large suspicion Patty would make good her threat, refuse to go home, and tag along with Nick wherever he might be heading. If he was too blind to see what was happening—Patty smiling so shyly into Doug Ledyard's eyes, using that poor boy mercilessly to rouse Nick's jealous passions for her—it was time somebody opened his eyes. And Nick was really responding, since she had stopped battering at his walls. It was as if he were opening his front gate a crack to see what lay out there that he might have overlooked.

Another thing that troubled her greatly, Doug Ledyard was falling like a pine in the forest. He wasn't saying much, but Patty was the only one he had eyes for. Ruby, in spite of her apparent good start, was definitely out in the cold. If Valerie could, she'd have shaken Patty until her teeth rattled—for all the good it would do, especially with Nick on her side at last.

"Okay, Val," he tossed at her, "you got it out of your system. 'Save' me some other time. How many times does a girl get to be eighteen? I say, let's give her a real bash. We owe it to ourselves!"

"Ah, Nick!" Patty's voice brimmed with feeling. "That's the sweetest thing you've ever done for me!"

"Sweet," Val echoed. "And very darned funny, if you ask me—"

"Which nobody is," he reminded her, his eyes crinkling with laughter.

"First you couldn't wait to get rid of us. But here you

are holding on for dear life to that—*hair shirt* of yours" He grinned sheepishly. She thought, he's as silly as any fifteen year old falling for the class glamour queen!

"I was just beginning to enjoy that particular kind of an itch, honey."

She rose up at once. "Don't you honey me. Just scratch away. It's your life!" She turned so awkwardly she fell against Ruby's shoulder, the jolt knocking the girl's mug from her hand. "I'm sorry," she apologized, beginning to mop the spill with her paper napkin.

Ruby's only response was a dead silence, and suddenly Val's frustration veered on her. "I *said* I was sorry. It was not done on purpose, *like some other things around here!*"

Crumbling the wet napkin to a soggy ball, she stuffed it into an empty mug and swept out. She had not missed the tightening of Ruby's jaw, or the further icing of those pale green eyes.

Not until she was well away did she realize how she was trembling, and that it was not from rage.

"A party," Val thought three days later, "is about the last thing I need!" She had been much alone for those days. Watching Patty turn that nice Ledyard boy into a chunk of putty was bad enough. But encountering Nick—Nick McKenzie of all people, wandering about with the look of a dying camel—was sending her straight up the wall.

There seemed no limit to the change in him. He had even—and she could barely believe her eyes when she saw it—gone and shaved off his beard. Only a neatly groomed wide sweep of mustache was left. The first time she'd run into him that way, she had stopped so abruptly to stare, there was nothing for it but to cover her reaction with a blunt, "Pulling out all stops, aren't you?"

He flashed back what had to be the whitest smile in the West. "Mad McKenzie stops at nothing." He chuckled. And she thought savagely, did he have to be that good-looking, too? But for the fraction of a second that their eyes met, bells rang deep in her consciousness, rendering her nerve-frayed and edgy.

"Like it? What do you think?" he asked, studying her.

"You're really askin' li'l me?" she began in her best Scarlett O'Hara drawl. "You wouldn't be carin' what poah li'l Valerie *thinks*, would y'all?" Then she whirled and started away, her heart racing.

"Hey!" he called after her, "I mean it. Do you like it?" There was an urgency in his tone that baffled her. Yet she would not pause or face him. She shouted back, "Would it matter?" and added before he could answer, "I know a couple of young women who would love to tell you first-hand."

She swept off, shaken more than she cared to admit. What was coming over him, preening like a cockatoo to win back what only a day or so before he'd been fending off? Idiot! Last night he had even played his damned fipple flute close enough to the cabin so that Patty, if she hadn't been sleeping like a baby, would have been pleased to know she had him where she wanted him.

Val had heard the music, too clearly. It was sweet, sweet to the point of pain. She had even caught herself shaping the words in her head . . . "And this shall be for music when no one else is near . . ." Until she realized what she was singing and blocked it out with a groan. "Thank you, Robert Louis Stevenson, I needed that!"

Val had suppressed a wicked desire to wake Patty and congratulate her. Or better still, to creep out and find Nick and deflate him with the news that the ears his efforts were intended for were buried in a pillow, and he was only making a nuisance of himself. She did neither. She resolved to sit back and let things happen which she could not prevent anyway. Patty would have her party because it had been promised. After that, no more excuses. They'd be off! Meanwhile, there'd been time enough for reflection—too much time—and a verse of a different order was running through her mind:

Once a fool, shame on thee.
Twice a fool, shame on me!

Yes, she acknowledged that now, while finishing the
repair on the patchwork skirt for the party. She acknowledged all the things that everyone had hinted at—that she
had refused blindly to accept because . . . because . . . there
is that "something" about a first love that defies all reason.
And when the mind cautions, "Watch it!" the heart will not
hear.

The heart brims over with excuses, explanations, alibis,
apologies. The heart says handily, "Let me type your college papers for you, darling" "Let me help with your re-
search." "Let me wake you in time for your early class."
"Let me . . . let me . . ." And eventually—because he was
ever ready to oblige—"Let me take your children, your very
own children off your hands, Barry, because you are much
too big and busy and important to be *burdened* with
them . . ."

The children were the only things she didn't regret. Remembering Gillian's warm moist kisses and Peter's bear-
cub hugs, she missed them, enough to shed a tear for them
still. But they were the only tears she'd shed, after all.

The hand-wringing was over. The absurd excuses for the
Ivy Ashleys in his life, and all those others who had sent
Claire into intensive therapy, were at an end.

For herself, the world was big and wide . . . and there
must be other men still to come down the pike. Good and
decent men, pleasant and interesting. Good-looking, too,
though that was not a requisite. Still, with black hair and
laughing eyes, wide of shoulder and lean-hipped, even
bearded, maybe! Dear God! What was she *thinking?* Not
like *him*; she didn't need that kind of a hassle . . .

Her thoughts took a sharp turn. Did she need *any* kind
of a hassle? Something had been troubling her since the
children had gone with Greg Drummond, and she'd finished
with Barry forever. A strange kind of malaise, an insecurity
about herself. She had had time to ponder, and she had

pondered with the starkest of honesty, and she had concluded that it seemed to be her fate to be a loser in love.
As far back as high school, the fellow she adored and *knew*
was going to ask her to the prom asked another girl, and
she did not get to go at all. In college, long before Barry,
she went with a sophomore whose face she could barely
recall now, but who had been her sun and moon and stars,
until she'd been eclipsed by a bosomy freshman and nearly
flunked a Chaucer course crying over it. Barry, of course,
she'd lost to Claire, and after the Ivy episode she had never
really trusted him again. It seemed that only the men she
had felt casual about wanted to hang around until she began
dodging their calls and avoiding them. For those men who
excited her, somehow life always provided another woman
to excite them more.

She was wary now. She realized with a flood of unease
how wary she'd grown. For instance, if Nick—not that she
cared that way for *him*, she was just using him for an
example, though there were things about him that, if he'd
only quit mocking her so stupidly, she just might come to
like him. A little. So if—suppose for a crazy moment he
meant a couple of the things he'd said lately, like that verbal
pass he'd made about his new beardless face, asking her
how *she* liked it—trying it on before asking Patty, of
course—but supposing he meant it, for the sake of argu-
ment. Supposing those brief times in his arms, on the trail,
in his cabin, had really gotten to him, a little . . .

In a wildly offbeat moment, she let her thoughts careen
crazily into that channel, shutting her eyes to blank out the
real world . . . Oh, but it wouldn't work. How long could
she hope to hold him? Good-looking as he was. And, okay,
nice in some ways, too . . .

About as long as she'd hung on to the fellow who left
for the bosomy freshman. She ended the fantasy, irritated
with herself.

What am I thinking? Asking for problems? For heartbreak? Haven't I had enough?

Rather for her The Rain Forest, and Simba the Sneak,

and Deedee, and safe, familiar things and people who would not leave her just because she loved them with all her heart.

She took a final stitch, bit off the thread, and shook out the skirt. Examining it, she abandoned the last of sentiment and went bristly again. You could hardly tell the skirt had been ripped, she thought, pleased. It would probably shake Ruby up a bit. For, of course, Ruby was to be at the party, too. Valerie had listened, incredulous, to Patty's sweet tones asking Ruby, "You will be here, won't you? I really, truly want you to come."

Ruby had stiffened as she always did with either of them, but Nick had said, "Of course, she's coming! Not only that, we'll ask a few others. Neighbors and such."

Val hadn't realized the Jordans *had* neighbors. But once again, she had been fooled by the distances. And in the past, when the country was being settled, didn't they always come together from miles around for any social event? And so it must be here now.

"You're not dressed yet!" Patty stuck her head in the door looking like the wide-eyed angel she definitely was not. She wore the same dirndl skirt in which she'd begun her "campaign" and the same peasant blouse. Valerie had packed everything else.

"I'll be dressed soon enough. I've been cleaning up around here. You know we're going in the morning, come hell or high water!"

"I know," Patty said softly.

Val shot her a suspicious look. "What on earth's come over you? Not that it's not a delight for a change. I've never known you so agreeable."

Patty threw her head back and sang, "I'm in love—with a wonderful guy!"

"What else is new?" Val sighed.

"Everything!"

Certainly the sparkle in her eyes was new. "Success is going to your head, my little dimwit cousin. How are you going to face tomorrow when it's all over?"

The girl's face seemed to fall, but only for an instant.

"I just won't think about it," she said, and turning, danced through the door.

Val felt dazed. Already she was dreading the morning, unless tonight Nick were to throw himself at Patty's feet and propose marriage! And the way things were going, he just might!

Grimly, reluctantly, she began changing for the party.

Chapter Fifteen

SHE HAD NOT counted on having a ball. Actually she was astonished to find herself dancing and enjoying it. At least a score of strangers had showed up, neighbors all, in a variety of vehicles from farm trucks to station wagons. Somehow a couple of carfuls of tourists had been waylaid and induced to join them, their faces reflecting their delight at this unexpected bonanza. Here and there people arrived singly on horseback, as did Ruby herself.

What startled Val and soured the scene somewhat was seeing Jake and Millie among them. But for this last night it was pointless to let that worry her.

In the center of the clearing, Nick and Doug had built a huge bonfire, most welcome in the chill night air, and readily available for barbecuing the steaks he had procured earlier from heaven knows how far afield.

There was music, too; at least half a dozen mouth organs and men to play them, wringing from them an almost unendurable sweetness. And there was Nick's recorder, or fipple flute as he insisted pedantically on calling it.

But mostly there was dancing, and the women's hair streaming on the wind, and their bright skirts twirling, their feet flying and their eyes flirting . . . with their lean-hipped, dungareed men in bold checkered shirts and ten-gallon hats, swaying with a grace that astounded Val as they spun her in their arms and sent her laughing down the line.

Not since her growing-up years had she square-danced, and here she was do-si-do-ing again, slipping with ease into all the old patterns, weaving in and out, handed from partner to partner, to be whirled and lifted and swung and caught and wheeled . . . and reeled . . . and suddenly without warning crushed so close in a huge pair of arms she gasped for breath! For a knifing moment, while her world rolled over, she caught the warm, familiar scent of him, woodsy with tobacco, and wool, and sweat . . . *intimate* . . . as that night on the trail. A gasp, half sob, fell from her lips. When he bent and pressed his mouth on hers, holding firm even while they danced, her knees went to water, and she sensed with horror she'd have dropped to the ground but for his arms around her. Straining back, she dragged her lips from his, found her footing again, and met his smile with a show of ice.

"What kind of a dumb step was that?" she hissed at him.

"Melt a little, honey," he murmured in her ear, holding her firm. "How'd you like to dance off in the dark, just us?"

Her voice shook ruinously as she said, "You're either drunk or delirious or both because we're leaving."

"Neither. We kind of owe each other—" He stopped, then plunged in haste. "Val, I like you. I mean, really."

"S-spare me," she managed in a whisper so thin, it missed entirely the contempt she had intended.

Then the music and the dance pattern parted them, and he laughed with a last lingering look as he passed her along to his sinewy successor, who doubtless wondered what it was that made this little gal shake so hard!

She was glad when the set ended and she found herself unexpectedly talking to Doug Ledyard. He seemed to have lost touch with Patty, though Val could have pointed her out edging close and closer still to Nick where he was throwing more wood on the fire and supervising the barbecuing. She smiled up at Doug, feeling a wave of sadness for him. He'd been so smitten with Patty, as so many young men before him, and she had led him a heartless chase, only to drop him...

"I figure I'd better be saying good-bye to you, Valerie, here, in case I miss you later. I'll be splitting very early tomorrow," he said.

"Oh, but so will we, Doug. We'll surely see you for a quick breakfast."

"Afraid not. I'll be leaving before dawn. I want a good early start, heading for Nevada, so I can beat the heat if possible. There are some areas I have to cover there before I pack it in and head back east. I've played long enough."

"Oh, but it's been wonderful meeting you, Doug. I'm glad you came."

"So am I, Valerie. It's been a real pleasure meeting you and—Patty."

His voice faltered at her name, and Valerie would have cheerfully spent the next six months kicking that child clear back to New York! He was such a sweet person. He didn't deserve what she'd done to him!

"Well, I wish you the best, Doug."

"Thank you. And the same to you, Val. Hope we meet again. Sometime..."

They shook hands warmly and he turned away. Valerie did not see him again. Not even later while she was helping to pass the food among the guests and joining in the feast herself. She wondered if Patty, having used him so badly, had at least had the decency to say good-bye before resuming her assault on Nick.

It was, however, mostly fun in spite of that. And in spite of another moment that gave her no joy—coming suddenly up behind Nick with his arm around Ruby's waist.

She was frankly bewildered, unless he was starting to give Patty a run for her money. But there they were together, Nick and Ruby, swaying to the music. She was so close she could not avoid catching their words.

"Happy, now, Ruby? Like it?"

"Oh, yes, Nick. I never dreamed—" she breathed.

"Well, you can dream now. Promise me you will. You'll never regret it, and remember, I'll never let you down."

Val did not wait. It was as if the ground shuddered beneath her. Less than half an hour earlier, he'd wanted to dance off in the bushes, telling her he *liked* her. How glad she was she hadn't fallen for *that* line. He'd be laughing his head off now.

With that, the party suddenly palled. She turned to slip away, and found herself barely a dozen feet from Jake Jordan.

Millie, beside him, seemed so absorbed in her daughter with Nick's arm around her, she was unaware of Val. But Jake made up for it. Across the narrow space he smiled, if lips pulled back from yellowed teeth could be called that. He took a step toward Val and she tensed.

"Reckon I'll be biddin' you good-bye, seein' as you'll be leavin' tomorrow," he drawled. It was so pointed, she thought, he might as well have added, "For your health, m'am!"

"Yes, we're leaving in the morning," she said coolly, then turned her back and walked swiftly from firelight to shadows. Her spirits sagged beyond all comprehension, but she took comfort in the thought that she would not have *him* to contend with again.

Before dawn she was awake. Something had penetrated her sleep, possibly Doug Ledyard's Jeep rumbling off in the darkness. But sleep would not come again.

Only images came, memories, which until this past night were no memories at all, only irritants. And what alchemy had transformed them into substance that could not be dispelled, she did not know, nor care to remember . . . a touch . . . a look . . . a grin . . . a kiss . . . a song . . .

Anyway, it was so much nonsense, the sort of thing that happens under a blazing Western sky . . . with a moon that should have been outlawed!

She stirred, wishing she had left some packing to do,

just to keep busy while Patty slept. Nick had brought the Jag close to the cabin, but Val hesitated to start carrying their bags to it and possibly wake Patty too soon.

The girl was sleeping like an infant. Val had heard her coming in, humming softly . . . *incredibly* it had struck her, since obviously her desperate little ploys for Nick had gained her nothing. She must know that. Any man who could stand in full view with his arm around another girl murmuring about dreams and promises was hardly hers for the taking. Or hardly worth having, she added, still chafing over her own encounter with him.

Why all the change in her? Where had all the sulking gone? Was she that good a loser? Could it be at long last she was growing up? If so, coming of age had its advantages, Val thought, and rose to tiptoe into the chilly dawn for a wash-up.

Patty was fully awake when she returned. So wide awake, Val wondered if she'd really been asleep before.

"You can grab some more sleep if you'd like," she told her.

"No, I'll start getting ready," Patty answered. "That way we can leave right after breakfast."

"Good. I hardly want anything much. Just coffee. We can stop somewhere later for breakfast."

"Fine, and I'll help you get the bags in the trunk after a bit."

Val marveled. To think she had been bracing for last-minute tears and pleas! The drive home might be fun after all.

"Wasn't last night terrific?" Patty sighed, taking a long stretch as she rose. "It was so beautiful. Nick really went to a lot of trouble to give me such a super eighteenth birthday. And even Ruby—the way she pitched in! I guess she was glad to be getting rid of me. I found it hard to believe."

Val's head was whirling. "I find so many things hard to believe I'd rather forget any of it ever happened. If you're going to wash up now, Patty, do. Nick must be awake. I'm sure I caught a whiff of coffee."

"Ready in a jiffy!" Patty called over her shoulder as she went.

The dawn was still veiled in mists when she returned and slipped hastily into blue jeans and a yellow turtleneck. Val, dressed for the road, was picking up small last-minute items to toss into her bag. "Let's stash everything in the car before we have coffee," she suggested.

"Oh can I do that later, Val?" Patty asked. "I'd—just like to see Nick, before anyone else is around—like Ruby, you know. I'd sort of like to say good-bye, and thanks, alone."

"Sure, go ahead," Val said. "It's not much. I'll handle it." She paused, and added thoughtfully, "I must say, Patty, you're taking it awfully well. I mean, not getting anywhere with Nick after all."

The girl turned and met her look head on. Then she shrugged lightheartedly. "Well, win a few, lose a few!" And finally with a smile that was truly tender, she added, "Thank you, Val, for everything."

"Everything?"

"For putting up with me. I'm sure it wasn't easy."

Val remembered that later. Just as she remembered that warmest of bright glows lighting the girl's face a fleeting moment before she turned and walked away into the eddying mists.

Val took her time after that carrying the bags out and arranging them in the trunk of the Jaguar to minimize knocking about. Finally thumping the lid down, she got behind the wheel and moved the car up closer to the trail. After that, she headed for coffee.

Patty's had all the time she needs for sentimental farewells, she thought. Ten or fifteen minutes had passed. The low-hanging fog was fast becoming less murky. She could see Nick's open door now, and realized with a sudden clutch at her middle she was not looking forward to this meeting. But he had done a great deal for her, she admitted reluctantly, and she would be gracious.

He was at the rough board table when she entered, riffling

through stacks of song sheets. He rose abruptly, almost nervously.

"It's—it's about time! Coffee's been ready for an hour."

"Sorry to've kept you waiting."

"Where's the princess?"

Valerie shot him a glance. "What?"

"Patty! Where the devil is she? Holding things up as usual?"

"Nick, stop playing games. Patty walked over here ten minutes ago. I saw her!"

He stared back, uncertain. "Come off it. I was sitting here all the time, door open and everything. Where'd she go?"

"Why, I don't know. I'll go out and call her. She might have stopped off to look at something."

"Like what?"

"How on earth do I know? I only said that she left the cabin ten minutes ago!" Val was annoyed clear through. It was a silly time for Patty to be dawdling; after getting up extra early, and begging a chance to talk alone with Nick. But it was much the sort of thing she always did—like following an inclination, perhaps, for a last look at the sunrise or whatever.

Out in the open, she shouted, "*Patty!* Come on! Coffee's waiting and we want to start!"

There was no response. Not even the chirrup of a nesting bird ruffled the profound silence. She walked off a little and called again in a new direction. And yet again. She quickened her step and hurried to the edge of the clearing and shouted some more. Soon she was flying from point to point, frustration having given way to bewilderment; and to harrowing doubt. Her voice had gone hoarse when she stopped dead in the center of the clearing feeling herself gripped in some surrealist dream! She swung around as Nick came striding up. Before he could ask "Where?" she cried, "I—don't *know*! She's—no place at all, she's vanished, Nick—v-vanished."

"All right, now, okay," he soothed, slipping an arm around her shoulder. "Calm down now. She's got to be around. People don't just vanish off the face of the earth . . ."

"Well, wh-where? It's not even misty anymore. Everything's crystal clear, and she's no place, no place at all!"

"Just take it easy. Come on back to the cabin. Sit down and have some coffee and relax."

Later, when he'd walked her there and sat her down with a steaming mug in front of her, she heard him mutter, "If this is that kid's idea of a lark, she is going to go home with marks on her bottom!"

Val was calmer now. "Nick, this is no lark. She was happy this morning. Happier than I ever saw her here. She—she'd given up on you."

"Took her long enough." His eyes grazed hers and looked away.

"But she did. She was all ready to go home. She especially wanted to thank you for the party and everything else. It's why she walked over while I was packing the bags—" She stopped abruptly. "Nick! The mine opening!"

He stared. "Hell, she wouldn't go prowling there. She knows the ground's full of cave-ins where they dug. I even heard her cautioning the kids once. But I'll have a look. No, you stay here. One of you's enough to worry about."

His voice, for all its denial, had faltered with doubt. Val, watching from the clearing, saw him pick up the brush-grown track that a hundred years past had served as a footpath up the slope, connecting the cabin site with the old aborted shaft. From where she stood, she could see the ancient timbers and rotted tree trunks, themselves half disguised by the growth of time.

There was no reason whatever for Patty to have gone that way. She had never shown the slightest interest in the place, and it was too preposterous to imagine a sudden overwhelming urge to explore it.

Watching Nick descend again, feeling carefully for firm terrain, she was prepared for disappointment.

"Nobody's been that way. Not a stone turned," he reported. "She'd have no reason anyway . . . I'm afraid, I don't know what to say . . ."

Valerie began trembling. "There's n-nothing to say, Nick—only that, somehow, P-patty has *disappeared!*"

Chapter Sixteen

HER EYES SWAM ABRUPTLY. Her hand flew to her mouth. She breathed, "Oh, Nick, I feel so helpless."

"Aw, Valerie, Valerie—" he murmured pulling her into his arms. They felt strong around her, and warm, buoying her immeasurably for the moment. Her head fell to his shoulder where after a time his fingers slipped through the dark rivers of her hair. "You can't come apart now, Val. Where's some of that old fight? There's just *got* to be some logical explanation. Listen, considering her track record, we'll give it a little more time, in case she *is* up to something. And then—"

He never finished. Together they turned to the sound of horse's hoofs pounding furiously up the trail. Valerie was still in Nick's arms when Ruby burst into the clearing, reining Sunny in sharply at sight of them. The horse skittered to a stop. Ruby urged it on again slowly, her face a mask, Val thought, as she neared.

"I thought you'd be gone by now," she said very low.

Nick's arms still hung about Val. "She would have been. There's been trouble. Patty's gone."

"Gone?"

"Disappeared. Oh—say, *you* didn't by chance see any trace of her along the trail?"

Ruby's mouth thinned. "I wasn't looking for her!"

"Ruby!" Nick sounded impatient. "This is no time for jealous peeves."

Her eyes dropped. "I'm not jealous of *her*! Anyway, I didn't see her."

Nick went thoughtful a moment. Finally, "We better take steps. We'll have to contact the authorities. The sheriff'll want to search the area. If nothing else, they can enlist the media—radio and TV—she's just got to be some-place, and the more people who are alerted the better the chance of finding her."

"Wait, Nick!" Valerie said. "The more people alerted, the sooner the news would carry back home. You *know* what would happen. The headlines:'New York Heiress Missing in Utah Wilderness'! Aunt Emily—I *can't* let her know that, yet. It would kill her!"

"But we can't take the chance of *not* knowing what's happening."

"You're right, Nick. But, please, just one more day?"

He went silent a time, then shrugged. "Okay, until to-morrow. Damn it! She can*not* have gone far! She's got to be here. We'll just keep looking. And you, Ruby, on your way back, keep a sharp eye out for anything, anything at all!"

The girl sat her horse without moving. "I wasn't going back, Nick. You said I should come."

He hesitated. "Yes. But you *see* this is no time, Ruby."

"Reckon it isn't," she muttered, wheeling Sunny.

"Wait," Nick called. "Ask your Dad to bring a couple more drums of water. We'll be short—if, if this hangs over any length of time."

The girl merely nodded and sent the horse into a canter around the cliff bend. When the last echoes had blended with the silence, Val murmured almost to herself, "She hates me."

"Now, Val, don't start that again." He sounded weary, straining for patience.

"Wasn't it plain how she felt? Finding me here when she expected to be alone with you. I'm not blind, Nick. I'm sorry I spoiled her fun. But I don't blame her, I know how I would have felt—" She could have bitten her tongue. It had slipped out, utterly without the meaning he promptly seized upon.

"Would you?" He asked it softly.

"Oh, damn it, you *know* what I meant," she said, reddening. "Ruby—"

"Ruby was disappointed, true. There were things we'd planned. But, Val, she doesn't hate you. Patty was her enemy, and for reasons not hard to understand."

"Of course not. Ruby's in love with you. Don't play dumb, Nick. Anybody she imagines in love with you is her enemy, and she hates them."

His lips quirked. "That includes you?"

"If that's what she imagines," she flared.

"Val—" He paused and the air was suddenly charged. "How's chances she's right?" She stared at him, her eyes narrowed. "Val?" He seemed suddenly bent on knowing. Her senses reeled, her mind scrambled. He was playing with her, and in a second she would cut him dead. Yet for just a moment longer she cherished the way his eyes rested on her, soft as a summer breeze . . . *Even if it was all an act!* "Is this a time for fun and games?" she snapped.

His brows shot up, and down again. "Okay, okay, back to Ruby and that good old-time paranoia. The 'she hates me' thing—"

"Damn it, Nick, don't you mock my judgment! If she doesn't hate me—" She hesitated. She hadn't meant ever to mention it, but he'd driven her, and suddenly it was out. "Why then did she deliberately take one of my skirts from my bag and—*r-rip it wide open!*"

"It wasn't deliberate!"

Her breath jammed. "Wh-what do you know about that?"

"Only what she told me. What she'd been agonizing about. Because she's so scared to death of you, she was too embarrassed to tell you herself. I urged her to. I told her you'd understand. But if she still hasn't done it, it's because she could not get up the nerve!"

"For what?"

"To admit that she was trying on your clothes. Ruby never *saw* clothes like yours and Patty's. She told me she knew you were busy with breakfast here and when she went to get that bundle of the kids' washing for her mother to do up, she just couldn't resist. Heck, Val, you're a woman. You've got to know what clothes like yours—all the New York styles—mean to a girl like Ruby!"

Val's eyes blinked against an unexpected sting at her lids. "Maybe," she conceded reluctantly.

"Well, then she heard you coming sooner than she'd expected. She said she yanked that skirt off so fast it ripped. She's bigger than you and I guess it was tighter around her hips or something. Anyway, she didn't have time to put it back or straight up your suitcase. She was so ashamed, she told me, she couldn't face you. And I believe her, Val. I only got it out of her when I realized something was bothering her enough to make her cry."

Almost against her will, recalling the way the girl seemed to skulk off when they met outside the cabin, Val believed her too. "Still," she said, "she might have said something to me later."

"You sure didn't make it easy for her, did you? You were mighty cool to her. And she sensed how you felt about her people."

"How?"

"Suspicious."

"With very good reason, Nick. When you've been glared at and—threatened."

"Threatened? Now who's got the wild imagination? Next you'll be blaming poor Jake for Patty's disappearance."

"No, not that. He was too anxious for us to leave. Why, only last night he was positively gleeful saying good-bye to me! And when he brought that last drum of water a few days ago, he told me very snidely indeed, 'Fore long,'"

—mimicking Jake's drawl—"'it'll be gettin' too hot for you 'round here.'"

"Oh, crumb! He meant the summer heat."

"He meant what he meant!"

"Whatever that means!"

"It means the man scares me! And he's no more anxious to be rid of me than I am of him! I thought this morning it would be over, and now—"

"Okay, okay," he said soothingly again as her tone edged into hysteria. "Listen, I insist you have some breakfast. Then I'm going to take a ride around these trails. I admit I can't conceive of any way she'd have gotten there. But I couldn't conceive of *anything* that little kook would do. So I'll be off and you can hold the fort—what's the matter? You're shaking all over."

She turned, hiding her face. But he pulled her around again. "What's wrong?"

"I'm scared, Nick. I can't help it. I'm just plain scared. I—I don't want to stay alone."

Once again his arms closed around her, and his big warm hand stroked her cheek until gradually her trembling subsided.

"Better now?"

"Yes. Much. I'm sorry."

"I'm not, I'll take as much as I can get," he mumbled so low she was not sure she'd heard. "All right, come along with me. We'll leave a note for Patty on my door in case she beats us back."

The search was every bit as fruitless as Val expected. She had a feeling Nick suggested it solely to be *doing* something. For hours they drove the surrounding trails, of which Nick knew many more than Val had suspected, occasionally stopping to question people in passing cars. He had the foresight to pack a lunch for the trail, but it was hardly the cheeriest of picnics. And when they emptied the thermos of coffee and she hinted at going back, he didn't protest.

By late afternoon, as they passed through the cleft in the

walls and entered the hidden trail, Val felt dazed. "I can't believe this is happening."

On the outer trail, close to the Jordan store, they passed Jake returning from delivering the fresh water drums. Millie was with him on the front seat, stiff and silent, in a way that Ruby was often stiff and silent; and it struck Valerie that perhaps she, too, felt the same needless and foolish inferiority with her.

"Sure sorry to hear about that little gal disappearin', " Jake said, his tone devoid of menace as usual when Nick was present. "Couldn't believe it when Ruby told us. Anything we can do, be sure'n let us know."

Val's hand clenched in her lap and she let Nick do the thanking for her. When he remarked, "Could anyone have been more sympathetic?" she did not trouble to answer.

They were almost to the clearing when she sniffed the air. "Smells funny—"

She saw his brow wrinkled. "If it were anyplace else, I'd say somebody was fixing for a barbecue. But it's—holy tomato!"

Nick braked with a screech. From the last of the cabins—Val's and Patty's— a column of smoke climbed upward staining the sky. Where they had slept the night before, there was nothing now but a mass of charred and smoldering wood with ripples of pale fire still visible among the ashes.

Numbed, speechless, they stared together through the windshield.

"Wh-what happened?" Nick finally muttered.

"I don't know," she breathed. "But Jake was here."

Chapter Seventeen

"IT *still* MAKES NO SENSE," he growled. "With or without Jake!"

"I know. But it'll have to do until you come up with a better explanation! And please don't forget how hot he told me it was going to get! Maybe now you'll stop defending him?"

Nick groaned and pulled the Land Rover in a little closer. Then he got down and sauntered to the ruins. Valerie came and stood beside him.

"Sure you didn't leave a burning cigarette this morning that could've been smoldering all along?"

"Did you ever see me smoke? Or Patty either? No, Nick, that won't do it."

"The wood was ancient, of course. And tinder dry. And the day was excessively hot!"

"And it's been waiting a hundred years for this precise day for spontaneous combustion to blow it!"

He went on staring until she added, "That fire was set, Nick!"

"Here we go again."

"I'm sure I smell gasoline. Somebody could have—"

He turned abruptly, his face showing exasperation, and

started for his own cabin. When she caught up, remarking how lucky it was she had moved the Jaguar out range, he acknowledged. "Yes. As it was, puzzling though it is, there wasn't anything much lost, really."

"Oh, nothing at all." She shrugged. "Just my sleeping quarters."

"Oh! Never thought of that. Well, we go back to Operation Full House. You get the cabin. I get the bedroll under the sky again."

She hesitated. "I don't like that."

"Then I get the cabin and you get the bedroll—or more sensibly, we both get the cabin."

"I don't like that, either."

"Give it a whirl, you might find you do." He said it lightly, but immediately his tone changed. A hush came over it, laced with urgency. "Val, it's not the worst thing that can happen. And there's nobody else now, is there?"

Her breath quickened. She went tense with wariness. She was not after any chance roll in the hay. "I—don't know what you're talking about," she stammered.

"You're not listening, are you, Val? You haven't been listening for days."

Ah, but she *had* been listening, if he only knew, to voices that spoke to her alone. Telling her, go ahead if you must, but it'll fall apart like all the rest. Go ahead, but you won't hang on for long, you never did. Go ahead, enjoy, enjoy, then cry your eyes out, plenty of time for that . . . Go on, don't say you weren't warned . . .

She drew a deep breath. "That's the craziest idea you've come up with yet," she said, her throat full, biting the words off and flinging them at him.

"Well! Thank *you*, m'am. Crazy, is it?" Now *he* was angry. Furious. "The way we two hit it off, the worst can happen we'll just kill each other."

"This is no time for humor, Nick," she reminded him.

"Who's laughing? Okay, back to Operation Full House. The cabin's all yours, the Star Hilton for me. Say when."

Rather early after darkness fell, it was time. The day's

awful suspense, the writhing torment of waiting for heaven alone knew what, topped finally by the mysterious blaze that gutted her cabin began taking its toll of body and nerves, in a way, Val suspected, that might even have been intended by its perpetrator.

If Nick could only see it that way. If he would just drop his absurd defense of Jake Jordan when everything pointed to him. But no, he was in such a foul mood that when she brought it up again over the light meal he prepared for them, he'd snarled at her, "You realize what a dumb thing you're saying, Valerie? They wanted to get rid of you so bad, they kidnapped Patty in order to keep you here longer!"

Her voice had gone scratchy with tears. "I didn't say that! I don't *know* what happened to Patty. I don't know if they had anything to do with that! But the cabin, are you going to tell me Jake didn't set it on fire? When we found it smoldering a short time after they'd been here?"

"But why? You haven't said why."

"Doesn't it look like a—*warning to me?* to get out?"

"Bunk! You've been seeing too much television!"

"And you, you're taking the whole thing too lightly. You just calmly accept everything that's happened around here as if it's perfectly normal any day of the week!"

His mouth set grimly a moment. Then he shoved his plate back, rose up, and went for his bedroll. "I think you need some sleep. I know damn well I do!"

She watched him stalk from the cabin without another word. Listening, she caught the rustle of his movements settling down in the dark, a rather comfortingly short distance off. After a time she walked over and shut the creaking door between them; and leaned on it a moment listening to the throbbing silence.

When finally she snuffed the last candle and lay shivering in the bunk, it was not from any chill. For the first time that day she was alone with terror. The enormity of Patty's disappearance came careening at her through the pitchy dark. The bewildering *purposelessness* of it! The where. The how. The why. And behind that always the menace to

herself. The creeping certainty that she had not seen the last
of whatever evil hunched with the patience of the jungle
to spring when *her* time should arrive . . .

Val huddled in her blanket roll. Sleep eluded her entirely.
The nameless threat beyond the cabin was suddenly there
within it. The shadows, black on black, seemed to vibrate
with it. A tendril of her own hair tickling her cheek brought
her bolt upright with a cry. Even when she knew what it
was, her body still shook uncontrollably and she could feel
the prickle of perspiration between her breasts.

The square of pale moonlight that marked the window
seemed to pulsate with a life of its own. When a passing
cloud blotted the light abruptly, like some great hand
slammed against the pane, she leaped to her feet and tore
to the heavy door. With a sob, she seized its handle and
heaved it ajar, its groaning protest crying out in the night.
She stood a terrified instant longer, scanning the scene while
her heart throbbed a tattoo at her temples. She raced for the
boulder and the hump beside it that was Nick's bedroll.

She was panting so audibly when she reached it, she
covered her mouth with a damp palm to keep from waking
him. That was the moment the moon chose to break free.
She stood a time breathing hard, uncertain what to do,
certain only that she could not return alone to the cabin!

She saw him stir, and knew all at once he was watching
her. That his eyes had been open all the time, that perhaps
they had not yet closed . . .

No word passed between. But all at once he flung back
the corner of his blanket and made room. With the barest
hesitation, she fell to her knees, then squirmed in beside
him. She was still trembling hard, though her robe wrapped
securely around her gown beneath a thick layer of blanket
should have shut out the chill.

But her trembling was suddenly of another sort. With
his arm around her, her throat locked tight. The warmth of
his body, its hardness, rocketed her back stunningly to that
night on the trail. She had not counted on it. She had not
been thinking in those terms, truly. It had been farthest

from her mind when terror sent her diving into his sleeping bag. Now her breath quivered, and she was afraid he might hear, and misconstrue, actually believe this was a ruse to be with him. Oh, but how could he, at a time like this— Patty and all . . .

At a time like this, what was his arm tightening around her for? And what was wrong with her, anyway, going so weak, limp? Why couldn't she stand up to his touch, get a grip on herself and keep her head screwed on straight?

This was meaningless, what he was doing, gathering her too, too close; shifting his body until every part of him met every part of her. It was meaningless, under the circumstances, and he should know it. It was leading nowhere. It was common animal sex and a tasteless time to unleash it.

His mouth brushed her cheek. She turned her head. It followed. She turned again, but he was too swift. His lips took hers with disarming directness. A sound lodged in her throat, a protest that never fully materialized. She drew a deep breath, and what followed was very like a sigh. She thought he would misunderstand, and he did. His free hand, tracing the curve of her hip, found the opening of her robe and entered tentatively. Her objection was a slight squirm that once again he deliberately misunderstood, she could tell. *This* was taking advantage.

"Hold me," he murmured. He sounded agitated.

"Nick, for God's sake, how could you—now?"

"Easy. Hold me, Val, honey."

She wriggled in his arms. "With Patty lying dead out there someplace, for all we know?"

"God rest her soul. Now hold me Val!"

"Not till Patty—"

"Hang Patty, anyway!" he erupted. "I don't believe there's a damn thing happened to her! She's pulling something! And Val, damn it, stop playing games. *You* know what you want. What I want. What we both want. Hell, why did you come here, anyway?"

She drew away, thrusting her fists at his chest. "Because

I was scared. And you darned well know it!"

"Malarkey! *This* is what you came for!" And he drew her beneath him and brought his weight upon her and kissed and kissed her until she begged for breath, and then he turned his back, leaving her half whimpering.

"I was—scared, honestly I was, N-Nick."

"Okay, *shut up!*" he growled. "Go to sleep. One of us might as well!"

Considering the foulness of his mood in the morning, he must hardly have slept at all. She was scarcely all sweetness and light herself. Chagrin at finding herself where she was unsettled her almost as badly as the flood of memories that followed. Appalled at finding her arm around him, she'd rolled away and jerked him awake.

"Thank *you!*" he muttered. "I was just finally catching a wink. What was all the panic? You're as chaste as when you came looking for me!"

She clenched her fists and answered in a rambling stream. "I did not come looking for you. I was scared to death and don't get carried away about your irresistible attractions—"

"Oh, shut up!"

She stalked off for a wash-up behind his cabin, her mind already dreading the day before them. When she returned, fully dressed, she said, "There's coffee perking."

"It better be good."

Her mouth fell open, preparing to suggest he make his own if he didn't like hers, when he added, "I was an idiot. I should never have listened to you. I should have gone straight to the authorities yesterday. I'm driving over to Jake's place after coffee. I'll call from there."

It swept through her mind she would be alone unless she went with him, and she'd heard no invitation—which did not especially surprise her, or shake her. Last night's terrors had seemed to dissipate with the mists of morning. There remained only the certain need to act now, even if acting meant what she had dreaded, having later to phone the terrible news to Aunt Emily.

Meanwhile, since Jake Jordan embodied everything she most loathed and feared, Val felt she would just as soon avoid the visit to his store.

"Sure you'll be all right?" Nick muttered later, preparing to leave.

"Yes, thank you, I feel much better," she said crisply. Then, not so crisply, "Are you going to be gone long?"

"No longer than I have to. I'll just make my call and do what they say, which I suspect will be to wait here until they send some men to check it out."

She watched the Land Rover rumble off past the point between the cliffs, listening until its last echoes sifted with the breeze. Turning slowly, she surveyed the desolateness that was Jordan's Hole, and for one staggering moment wished she had ridden with him.

The silence was immediately eerie, especially with the last of the patchy mist still circling along the ground. It shot through her head abruptly: this was precisely the hour that yesterday she had watched Patty walk into their coiling arms . . . and never come out . . .

She stood a long time in the center of the clearing staring before her. She could feel the skin along her arms prickling, and a dampness form on her brow and upper lip. She wanted to move, to hurry back to the shelter of Nick's cabin where there were things that were real, solid, familiar. His heavy hiking boots. His flannel shirts suspended from the same pegs that a century before had held other men's clothing. His sheafs of paper, his books, his typewriter, his pipes, his . . . aroma . . .

She could not move a muscle. She felt gripped by the same terror of the night before. Even when the morning was finally blue and cloudless, with the first shafts of sunlight fingering their way down along the slopes backing the old shaft, she could not budge.

It seemed to her half an hour must have passed before

she heard the rumble of a motor. Relief broke over her so violently, she grabbed for her heart and went faint. Nick was back for something. He could not have made it to the Jordan's and returned, but whatever he'd come back for, he was here! And reeling a little she began running, *flying* toward the mouth of the trail.

She reached it precisely as the front wheels turned the second to last bend—and there she froze!

It was the rusting old pickup truck. Jake Jordan's. With Jake behind the wheel. And beside him, staring dully before her, Millie, his wife.

Chapter Eighteen

VERY SLOWLY, VALERIE backed away, making room for the truck as it began to enter the clearing.

Jake's yellowed smile as he passed her came as a secondary shock wave. Even Millie's expressionless nod failed to lift the pall of fear that threatened any moment to suffocate her.

When the truck had rolled to a stop, Jake leaned out and called, "Where's McKenzie?"

A trick, she knew. "You must have seen him. He was on his way to your store."

"Was he? Well, we jus' come 'round the other way. Had to drive south a ways to pick up some supplies. Got the mail 'long with it. Brought him his, long as we was passin'."

For a second, she felt some shred of hope that he might just leave the mail and go. But as he handed down Nick's letters, all at once he spotted the burned-out cabin.

"Hey-y now! What could 'a happened there?"

Valerie slipped the letters into her jacket pocket, trying not to glare too hard as she murmured, "Funny, I was wondering if *you* might know, since it happened right after you were here yesterday."

If he heard, Jake gave no sign. But descending from the truck, he stood a moment sizing up the ruins.

"Ain't you comin', Jake?" Millie asked querulously. "Ruby's all alone up at the store."

"She ain't likely to get trampled to death in any rush," he grumbled. "I wanna take a look."

"T'aint nothing to see 'cept a burnt-out old shack," she whined, shifting irritably on the seat. Val, watching her, was suddenly aware of Jake's rifle gleaming across the back ledge of the seat. It was a jolt she could have done without at the moment.

The woman's sullen eyes followed her husband as he ambled across the clearing, ignoring her. When he reached the cabin site, she shoved a bedraggled lock behind her ear irritably and mumbled, "Don't know what he 'spects to find. Messin' 'round where he's got no business."

Privately, Val wondered if he wasn't actually hoping to find and *hide* something, some clue perhaps to how the fire had been set—by himself, naturally.

"It's lonesome up here," Millie volunteered unexpectedly, her tone so subtly altered, Val's eyes came slowly to her face. She was staring at Nick's cabin when she added, "Don't it bother you none, bein' up here all alone?"

"You mean because of the things that have happened?"

The woman seemed to hesitate. Her gaze remained intent on the cabin. "Bein' all alone, I'm meanin', with *him!*"

Val's breath sucked in sharply. "Mr. McKenzie is a gentleman. Furthermore, he treats me like a lady."

Millie's eyes avoided hers. "He treats Ruby like a lady, too, miss. That's because she is one. And the way she been raised, she wouldn't be spendin' no nights with any man, lest he married her first."

Val was too stunned to be offended. She spoke up curtly. "I assure you, Mrs. Jordan, I would not even *be* here now if my cousin hadn't disappeared. And I cannot and will not leave until she's found again! And if that means spending nights, as you put it, with Mr. McKenzie, then that's what it must be."

Millie's face hardened perceptibly, her mouth dipping at the corners. After a tense pause, she asked, "Where you been lookin' for her? You looked up there yet?"

"The mine mouth? Of course. Mr. McKenzie found nothing to indicate she'd been anywhere near it. Besides, there's no reason why she'd have gone there in the first place."

"She done a lot of things nobody had no reason for. Besides, I wasn't meanin' the mine. I was meanin' up there."

She flung a bony sun-dried arm to the gentle rise back of the shaft site. From the clearing, only the near edge of what was evidently a plateau was visible. What lay beyond, Val suddenly realized, was anybody's guess. But even as she wondered why on earth Patty would have climbed that far, Millie muttered, "She could 'a gone to get a look at the sunrise or somep'n. It's beautiful up there. When Jake and I was courtin'—" She stopped.

Val wasn't listening anyway. Excitement had begun to clamor. Patty had spoken of the beauty of the place. Could it be that in those last minutes the impulsive and wholly unpredictable girl had decided on a quick look around? Perhaps she'd been there before, avoiding the mine entrance itself. It really could be done. And yet—

"What could have happened to her if she did go up there?"

Millie shrugged. "Who knows? The girl mighta got faint or somep'n. She could 'a stepped in a hole runnin' and broke a leg. She might be layin' there yet waitin' for someone to find her. If she is, she's a-sufferin', I can tell you. The sun gets almighty hot up there these days..."

Val stood transfixed, gazing at the near horizon of the plateau.

"I think I'll go and look," she said abruptly.

"Sure would if I was you," Millie agreed. "Won't take you but a few minutes to find out."

Jake was still poking around amid the charred beams when she hurried to the brush-grown trail that Nick had used the previous day. It was not too steep a climb, but remembering how he had picked his way, she took the greatest of care to keep from stepping into some unseen hole which, as Millie said, might well have been Patty's fate. Valerie shuddered and exerted herself faster at thought of the girl possibly lying out in yesterday's broiling sun, severely injured, possibly delirious from thirst and pain. Even this early the sun was warming swiftly. Today could be as fierce as the day before. "Oh, God, if she's there let her be alive!" she prayed, climbing. "And let me find her before Jake leaves, so he can help me bring her down."

Nick might well be returning by now, but what if he weren't?

So certain she was, by the time she passed the mine entrance, that Patty had gone this way before, she marveled that Nick hadn't thought of it. The girl had disappeared in a matter of minutes, about the length of time it was taking Valerie to climb the last of the rise before the terrain would level off. She glanced down once. Millie was watching her, shading her eyes from the sun. Jake hadn't noticed, apparently, for he was down on his knees, still poking around the embers.

Valerie paused for breath at the very crest of the rise. The lay of the land surprised her somewhat. It seemed far more arid than the slope below, accounting no doubt for the thinning of the growth. But everywhere she looked lay huge boulders, or clusters of sizable rocks, tossed there perhaps in some ancient volcanic turbulence; all casting long lines of shade before the still low-lying sun. With a spurt of hope, Valerie realized Patty might well be lying anywhere among them, and started to search. Her last backward glance over the lip of the plateau picked out Millie, still shading her eyes, and a blur of motion where Jake stood. She thought she heard him shout something thinly, to Millie. But she was far too excited to concern herself.

She proceeded, less warily since the going was easier. Twice, three times she shouted Patty's name. And as she moved along, drawn by clumps of brush skirting larger clumps of rock, she shouted again and again. Even with no response, hope refused to die. For there was still so much ground to cover.

She glanced at her watch, wondering if Jake was still

there; or better still, if Nick had returned. Ten minutes had passed since her last look below, then fifteen, and still she wandered in the uncomfortable heat. She thought to move back to the plateau's rim, but a larger formation of rock casting a swiftly foreshortening shadow caught her attention. Something . . . some movement . . .

Some sound! She was sure she'd heard it—and seen at a distance of perhaps thirty feet a faint quivering in the dusty brush!

"Patty!" she shouted and hurried forward. She had halved the distance, when she froze!

Horror seized her. With a fear that denied every other fear she'd ever known, she watched the thing lift its flat and ugly head above a loose S-shaped curve. She was close enough, she could see its bifid tongue darting in and out, in and out . . .

Never before had she seen one, but she knew what it was. Knew what was meant by the hiss of its horny tail. And she was paralyzed. She could not move a finger, until a new sound at her back abruptly sent her into panic. Was it another? Was it a nest? She whirled, falling back—and looked squarely into the muzzle of Jake Jordan's rifle!

In the split second before the world exploded around her, she sensed the setup!

Chapter Nineteen

AT FIRST IT was a gentle swaying motion that went on and on . . . And then there was a sound. a whisper, a murmur . . . Her name floating on its surface . . .

"Valerie . . . oh, Val, honey . . . You're all right . . . You'll be fine now . . ."

It could not be. Nick was only in heaven. And she'd just walked the plains of hell.

"Okay, okay, sweetheart let me get you down to the cabin where there's water. You'll be fine in a while."

"Oo-ooh, Nick," she breathed and nestled against him. If it was fantasy, let it be for a time. "Nick, am I bleeding much?"

"B-bleeding. Why in hell would you be bleeding?"

Yes, she sighed, *that* was Nick! "Because—Jake shot me. I always told you. Am I—am I going to live?"

He chuckled. She could feel his chest heaving with silent laughter. "Dumb, stubborn, beautiful girl. I'm through fighting it. Maybe it's half the reason I love—never mind that now. Listen, if Jake hadn't shot, you'd be writhing in agony this minute, if you lasted this long! Thank your lucky stars Jake's the crack shot he is or that rattler hissing at you

from under that rock would have gotten you before you
knew what happened!"

"R-rattler?" She remembered then.

"Yes, rattler. Like in snake. He was only about ten feet
from you when Jake got him. Those babies have a long
stretch, too."

Her breath filtered away slowly. "I—saw something
move. I thought it might be Patty, Millie said—"

Immediately from behind them, as Nick trudged down
the slope, came a gruff, "I'll fix *her* wagon!"

"Is that Jake?" she whispered against Nick's chest.

"Darn right. He's behind us. I followed him up here.
Came driving in in time to see him going up the slope like
a bat out of a cave! When I didn't see you, I knew, even
without asking Millie who wasn't doing much talking by
then."

From behind them again, Jake growled. "She done all
the talkin' she's a'goin' to do for the next hun'erd years,
I can promise you that."

"M-Millie? But why would she do that to me?"

"Fool ol' woman!" Jake snarled and no more was said
until Nick finally set her on her feet in the clearing.

"You feel better?" His voice was softer than she'd ever
heard it. She nodded, smiling up beneath her lashes. "I'm
sorry, for all this fuss."

"You should be," he murmured, his arm still around her
waist. "You've been warned about going up there. Why'd
you listen to her?"

"It sounded so reasonable, the way she put it, Nick..."

She broke off as from the vicinity of Jake's truck voices
flared.

"Why in hell did you send that gal up that way? You
know the place is a snake pit!"

Millie stared as if carved of stone, her eyes dull, lifeless.
Until suddenly Jake added, "And why'd you pour that gasoline on them rags and set 'em on fire, while I was busy
carryin' in them water drums? Don't think I don't know,
even if they didn't catch enough for me to notice before we

left here yesterday! You can still smell the stuff and I found a scrap of them greasy rags I keep in the truck. And the gas can's near empty! And I got a notion you slit the lady's fanbelt that day she come by, didn't you, old woman? While I was off showin' her the outhouse for the young 'uns."

Abruptly she exploded, her eyes gone fiery. "You know I had to! You know what was goin' on and why I had to do it! You didn't even *try* to keep her away. That little blond was bad enough but this one—"

"Shut up, ol' woman! I tried all I was goin' to try. And I don't want nothin' so bad I'd try any rotten tricks on a lady with two kids just to get it! You been stirrin' up all the trouble you could ever since she come. Don't deny it, woman! I ain't dumb!"

"No," she spat, "you ain't dumb, Jake, you're just lazy." Val saw her expression go from sullen to bitter. "Lazy, that's what you are. If you weren't, we'd'a had a lot better livin' than what we got."

"You complainin'?"

"Not for me, I ain't. It's too late for me. But what's Ruby got to look ahead to, hey? I was just as pretty as her once, and you know it, Jake! You think I want her endin' up lookin' like me? Livin' like me? With never anything like these girls got? Or mos' any other girls? The clothes, the travelin', the nice times and—"

"What's all that got to do with the way you been actin'?"

"—*and a decent man!* That's what, Jake! It was her one chance in a lifetime. She was gettin' along fine, till they come along and spoilt it for her—*spoilt it!*"

"You're talkin' crazy talk, Millie!"

"No, I ain't. I know what I'm talkin'. Ruby—she loved him, and he—he was mighty nice to her, too, till they got here. All I could do was try to stop her—*that* one—from comin', 'cause he wasn't much for the other one! But *her*—"

Jake took a menacing step toward the truck, and she went still. "Listen here," he said, "you tell me, and tell me straight—you have anything to do with that little gal bein' lost?"

"Oh, no! Jake, no!" she protested, her bitterness draining. "I don't know what happened to 'er. I was only glad they was goin'. Why would I've tried to keep her here longer?"

Jake turned a haggard face to where Nick held Valerie close in his arms. "Guess I got to 'pologize for her. Don't know what else to tell you."

As he started climbing into the truck, Val hurried forward. "*I* must apologize to *you*, Jake. I surely misjudged you. I was never so wrong about anybody in my life."

He looked down a moment. "Can't say as I blame you, miss."

But Val's last glance was for Millie, rigid in the seat beside him, looking neither to right nor left, as two trickles of tears formed crooked trails down her seamed and dusty cheeks.

Val stood without moving as Jake turned the truck and nosed it around the bend. When Nick came up behind her, she murmured, "I feel so sorry for her, I could cry." And after a moment, "For Ruby, too, I guess."

"You needn't for Ruby," he said, slipping an arm around her waist again.

"Oh?" She stiffened a trifle. "You've got—plans for Ruby?"

"I had," he said soberly. "They're Ruby's own plans now. It was half the reason for the party, Val. I wanted that girl to see what could be done with this place. I wanted her to understand. It'll mean hard work, first to dress up the store and the buildings around it that could so easily become a small motor inn for a start. Eventually right here, these cabins could be converted into a rough-it type of camp. For horseback riding, and bonfires at night, and dancing, and a good living. And one day, when she's alone, she just might find herself, if not rich, at least a happy, independent woman. If she needs starting money, I told her I'd lend it to her. I'd consider it a good investment. At least I made her promise she'd try—"

"So *that's* what I heard," Val murmured, remembering

that grossly misunderstood little scene at Patty's party. "But Nick..." She paused, then went ahead again as if she had to know. "You were in love with her, a little, weren't you?"

"I like her a lot," he said with candor. "From the day I first stopped at their store and glimpsed her hanging a washing out back, singing one of those melodies I'd never been able to find the words to. She actually ran and hid when I tried talking to her, until Millie made her come and talk. And talking led to this place, especially when I mentioned to Jake I'd like to hang around for a while. After a few days, she began being at ease with me. And yes, I like her. She's a fine girl. The teacher in me saw her potential. That's a long way, however, from love."

"Did she know that, Nick? She certainly seemed in love with you."

"She may have thought so for a time. Because I was trying awfully hard to make her realize how worthwhile she is. It wasn't right that she should go to waste, as Millie said. But what she was really in love with, I'm absolutely certain, was everything I represented. The whole wide world beyond her narrow canyon. Right now, I think she's finally at long last in love with her future. And if some time you'd sort of bolster her courage about that and show her you understand about everything that happened, I'm sure it would help her enormously. Anyway, you'll certainly want to have a talk with her before you go?"

"Yes, I do. I misjudged her too, badly. But, Nick, before I go? What about the sheriff? What did he say?"

"The sheriff and his men should be along any minute. We can only wait. Let's have some coffee."

They were walking slowly, disconsolately toward the cabin, when Valerie felt the mail in her jacket pocket. "Oh, almost forgot. Jake dropped these off for you."

She handed them over and went inside. She was just striking a match to the camp burner when Nick shouted, "That creepy, rotten kid! Val! Look!"

She went flying through the door. "Is—is she back?"

His eyes were virtually bulging. His hand shook holding

out a letter. He roared, "I wish she were here! I'd tan her so hard her grandmothers for thirty-six generations past would shudder in their graves!"

"It's from Patty!" she cried.

"Not at all! Nothing like that! It is—if you can believe it—from Mr. And Mrs. Douglas Ledyard the Third! On their honeymoon! In Las Vegas! Where they headed after she sneaked off to meet him waiting for her up the trail in his Jeep! Can you believe that? I swear I'm going to flunk Ledyard the next time he shows up in my class!"

She snatched the letter from him. But her hand shook so badly she could barely read Patty's childish scrawl. Nick grabbed it back and read it aloud, mimicking Doug's low rumbling voice, telling how sorry he was to have worried them, but Patty, whom he adored, had warned him if they announced their plans, Valerie would give them a hard time.

"And I would have! What could I tell her mother? I was responsible for her!"

"She's her own woman now, honey." Nick grinned. "Why do you think she waited until she turned eighteen?"

"Well, I certainly would have tried to make them wait. But I should have guessed. I was so dense! She dropped so many hints. She was in such great spirits, even when it was plain to me she wasn't getting anywhere with you! She even—thanked me for putting up with her, as if something final was going to happen. Now I just hope it works."

"Listen to *her*, then. 'My dearest Val, You're going to laugh, but I never loved anyone in all my life, not even Nick who's sweet but kind of old'—Bite your tongue, Mrs. Ledyard—'the way I love Doug. I knew it the moment I saw him, and he did too. I had to play it cool and pretend he didn't mean anything to me until we could get away, of course. We planned everything down to the minute, while you were still imagining I was after Nick, and that I was only using my darling Doug to make Nick jealous. When Doug's Jeep left real early, I could have gone with him, but you'd have guessed and run us down before we could get to Nevada to be married. Forgive me. I've never been so happy in my life. I've spoken to Mother on the phone and reminded her it's exactly what she did with Daddy! We're working our way east in time for Doug's next semester at school. I hope all goes well with you and that you've finally come to your senses and stopped pretending'"—Nick's voice started coming apart—"'stopped pretending you're not head over heels in love with Nick McKenzie!'"

He finished with a grin. "Well, well! More to that kid than I gave her credit for. She's one bright girl!"

"With one large imagination!" Valerie flared, flushing deeply, but sounding breathless. "I'm feeling sorry for Doug already."

"Not me. Must be nice having a woman who's not afraid to say what's in her heart!"

She turned and walked off a little, but he tagged after her, speaking in the same breath. "Rather than one of those disappointed-in-love types, who'd rather be alone all her life than take a second chance."

She turned to face him. She could go no further, unless she walked through the side of the cabin. "Do you *really* know what you're trying to say?"

His face went taut a moment. "I do. And you damn well do, too, Valerie. You knew, or you should have, the night I suggested Patty's party."

"I thought you said that was just so Ruby would see what it could be like."

"That was *half* the reason, I told you. The other half— I guess I hoped you'd stay on a little longer. I was idiot enough to think that with Barry out of the running . . . Well, I figured I couldn't have been that wrong about what we were feeling that night on the trail, and after. I thought, why not? Damn it, I even shaved off my beard so you'd really see what you'd be getting, and that was no small sacrifice."

He'd moved in so close, her back was flat against the cabin. She thought he would touch her. Suddenly she wanted him to very much but he hesitated. "I knew how I felt,

Val. And you had to know, too. You're not dense. Val,
you've been wanting me every bit as much as I've been
wanting you, want you now. And will go on wanting you
while there's blood in my veins. That night on the trail, if
I hadn't opened my big mouth and gotten into some kind
of philosophical discussion about how much we wanted
each other, we'd have *had* each other, damn it, right then,
Val!" His tone underwent a change. "You know what I'm
trying to say? Look at me, Val."

She looked, and her widening eyes grew eloquent with
"what he was trying to say."

Gone suddenly were the doubts, the tormenting insecur-
ities that past failures had left in their trail. Failures that in
a flash had become ludicrously insignificant. For this was
different; she knew it. She read it in his face, his eyes. This
was something that had never been; fresh as a new morning.
Different because *he* was different, different from any man
who had walked through her life before. *And this was forever*.

Her eyes gazing back filled suddenly with tears, and with
laughter.

"You've got it!" he whispered. "I love you, Val. I *love
you*. I don't know any other way to say it. Is that plain
enough? Or must I play it for you?"

"No, oh no, Nick. There won't be time. Just kiss me,
that's music enough—quick, for heaven's sake, before the
sheriff's boys find us like this."

He seized her, and with a throaty chuckle said, "that's
not all they're going to find."

His mouth devouring hers, she'd have sworn she heard
it again, filling her heart as once it had filled the night...

"And this shall be for music when no one else is
near,
The fine song for singing, the rare song to hear!
That only I remember, that only you admire,
Of the broad road that stretches and the roadside
fire...."

Introducing a unique new concept in romance novels!
Every woman deserves a...

Second Chance at Love

You'll revel in the settings, you'll delight in the
heroines, you may even fall in love with the
magnetic men you meet in the pages of...

Second Chance at Love

Look for three new
novels of lovers lost and found coming every
month from Jove! Available now:

___ 05907-2 ALOHA YESTERDAY (#10) $1.75
     by Meredith Kingston

✓ 05638-3 MOONFIRE MELODY (#11) $1.75
     by Lily Bradford

___ 06132-8 MEETING WITH THE PAST (#12) $1.75
     by Caroline Halter